The Fourth Stall

BY Chris Rylander

SCHOLASTIC INC.
New York Toronto London Auckland
Sydney Mexico City New Delhi Hong Kong

ISBN 978-0-545-44549-8

Copyright © 2011 by Chris Rylander.
All rights reserved. Published by Scholastic Inc.,
557 Broadway, New York, NY 10012, by arrangement with
HarperCollins Children's Books, a division of HarperCollins
Publishers. SCHOLASTIC and associated logos are
trademarks and/or registered trademarks
of Scholastic Inc.

12 11 10 9 8 7 6 5 4 3 2 1   12 13 14 15 16 17/0

Printed in the U.S.A.   40

First Scholastic printing, January 2012

For Amanda, we're going to live forever

Chapter 1

You need something?

I can get it for you.

You have a problem?

I can solve it.

That's why they come to me. By "they" I mean every kid in the school. First graders up to eighth graders. Everyone comes to me for help, and most of the time I'm happy to provide it. For a small fee of course.

My office is located in the East Wing boys' bathroom, fourth stall from the high window. My office hours are during early recess, lunch, and afternoon recess.

Sometimes I do pro bono work. I don't know why free is called pro bono, but it is. If your situation seems important enough, I just may offer my services without the usual fees of money or favors. But that doesn't happen too often. And when it does, it's usually because Vince asks me to.

Vince is my best friend and right-hand man. He's a good guy; in addition to being awesome with numbers he's also the most book-smart kid I know, and the best business manager a guy could have. We started this business together, so when he gives me one of those looks that only I know, that says, *Hey, Mac, you should cut this kid a break and do this one pro bono,* I listen to him. I know you shouldn't mix your business and personal life, but we run a tight operation and have been friends since kindergarten.

My real name is Christian Barrett, but everyone calls me Mac. Mac is short for MacGyver. This eighth grader, Billy Benson, called me that once, and it stuck. Now it's just Mac, because people are lazy.

Right now you might be wondering how a little blue-eyed sixth grader with shaggy dark brown hair could end up with a business like this? And I don't blame you—I hardly believe it myself sometimes. It's actually a pretty long story that's probably best left for later. So for now let's just say it involves an old trailer park playground, a vampire, and one angry fourth grader and we'll leave it at that.

Anyways, I mostly handle easy stuff, like getting kids

test answers, or forged hall passes and doctor's notes, or video games that their parents won't let them play, but every once in a while something tough comes my way. Like my last client on this particular Monday. His was one of the most difficult problems I ever faced.

I was sitting behind my desk in the fourth stall from the high window. Maybe I should stop here to explain how we fit my desk into the stall. A lot of kids will tell you that the toilet was cleared out years ago due to a huge accident. They say some joker tried to flush a whole box of Black Cats and four cherry bombs down the toilet. Supposedly, the porcelain shards exploded everywhere and severed his arm and he now has a hook for a hand and lives in some special institution for kids who think they're pirates.

I know the truth, though, because I have connections the other kids don't. The toilet was removed when some kid figured out Principal Dickerson's bathroom schedule. Apparently, old people use the bathroom at the same time every day, and this kid, Jimmy Snickers, found out that Principal Dickerson used the fourth stall from the high window in the East Wing bathroom every single day at 12:02. Always. Why did he use that exact toilet? Maybe it was because the fourth stall from the high window was the biggest stall in the bathroom and had handrails that he needed to use because he was so old? I really have no idea. I know a lot of stuff about this school, but some things are just a mystery, and are meant to stay that way.

Anyways, one day during morning recess Jimmy brought six bottles of industrial superglue into the fourth stall from the high window. Now, Jimmy was a pretty clever kid, so he knew that simply supergluing Dickerson's butt cheeks to the seat was not enough, because the seat could easily be removed with just a simple wrench. Instead he lathered up not only the seat but also the screws and joints holding the seat to the toilet bowl itself. The concoction of glues he created, combined with years of built-up pee and rust and gunk, bonded together like the most stinky, sticky cement ever invented. Principal Dickerson wasn't going anywhere.

Dickerson didn't yell for help because it would have been embarrassing to be found by a student. So instead he waited. And waited. And waited. Eventually the janitor found him at five o'clock that evening. Even though at that point Dickerson was really hungry from missing lunch, at least he was able to use the bathroom. They had to call in plumbers to remove the entire toilet and ship both Dickerson and his new porcelain shorts to the hospital, where doctors were able to surgically separate the two.

Dickerson never ordered a new toilet because the process of doing so would just bring unwanted attention to the whole embarrassing ordeal. That, and the school had spent most of its money that year buying these cool Nike uniforms and tracksuits for all the sports teams. Then by the following year the kids and teachers probably just forgot all about the missing toilet, which was fine with Dickerson. So the fourth stall from the high window remained toilet-less and became the perfect place for my office. Mostly because it was in the farthest reaches of the school's East Wing where there were no classrooms, except for a rarely used band room.

The bathroom was also secure and private due to an arrangement I had with the school janitor. In fact, he had even given me a key so I could lock up the bathroom during nonbusiness hours to keep kids from coming in and messing with my stuff. Maybe I'll get into that arrangement more later on, but for now I should probably get back to the story at hand.

So where was I anyway? Oh yeah, Monday. It was lunchtime. I was sitting behind the desk my crew had installed in the fourth stall. Business had been a little slower than usual the past couple of days, but otherwise it had been just another normal day at the office up to that point. Joe, my strongman, stood outside the bathroom, forming lines and regulating the flow of kids. Only one customer was allowed inside the bathroom at any given time. Joe also kept out any unwanted company. He was an eighth grader, the biggest kid at our school; he towered over the other students like an NBA player at a midget convention. No one messed with Joe, not even me. But he was loyal, and I compensated him well.

Joe ushered in kid after kid, first come first serve. Vince was the only person other than me and the client allowed inside the bathroom when we were seeing customers. He usually stood outside my office, where he patted the kids down and checked for recording devices, stink bombs, or other undesirables.

The second-to-last client of that afternoon was a big football player named Robert Hoveskeland. He looked funny sitting in the small plastic chair in the cramped stall. His huge knees were almost level with his shoulders. I had a good feeling about the kid right away, probably because he was wearing a Chicago Cubs jersey.

"What can I do for you, Robert?" I asked. "Need more playing time? Less playing time? A girlfriend? Help breaking up with a girlfriend?"

"No, not exactly," he said.

"It has to do with a girl, though, right?"

He nodded and I thought I saw him blush a little bit.

"I want to take a girl to that new movie *Idiots Doing Stupid Stunts*, but I don't know how to get us in. It's rated R. My dad's a cop and he's obsessed with the whole 'the law is the law' thing, so he won't go for it.

Anyways, I already told her I could get us in, so I'm just wondering if you could help me somehow. I don't want her to think I'm a liar."

"I think I can help you, Robert. When were you two planning on going?" I asked.

"Well, I invited her to go Saturday night. This Saturday."

"I need a few moments please," I said.

I saw him shift uncomfortably in the small chair as I looked through my Books. My Books were a few notebooks that I used to keep record of customers and their requests, such as who owed me favors and other stuff like that. I also kept a record of all my connections, like people who could get me stuff that most kids didn't have access to. Such as Vince's older brother Victor. We used him to get us stuff that only eighteen-year-olds can buy. Vince kept his own Books, too, but his dealt more with how much money we had and who owed us money and other financial stuff like that. I checked my Books for the problem at hand. I knew a guy at the theater who owed me a favor, but he didn't work on Saturday. I hoped Robert would be flexible.

"Okay, Robert, here's the deal: I can get you two in but not Saturday night. Do you think she'd agree to go Friday instead?"

"Yeah, I think so," he said as he scratched the back of his head.

"Good, just tell her you have to babysit your little brother or something on Saturday; that usually works. Look for a cashier named Derrick; he's tall and has short dark hair. He'll be expecting you. Sound good?"

"Yeah, except that I don't have any little brothers or sisters. So I don't know what—"

"Robert, Robert, Robert. Use your imagination. Tell her you have to go out for your mom's birthday on Saturday or something. It's okay, everybody can tell a harmless lie once in a while. Right?"

He hesitated. I could tell that he was a good guy because he seemed to be such a terrible liar.

"Yeah, okay, I can do that. What do I owe you?" he finally said.

"Tell you what, I didn't fix your problem perfectly, plus you're a Cubs fan, so we'll do it at a discount. How does five dollars and a small favor sound?"

"A favor?" he asked.

"Yeah, there may be a time when I need your help with something. Don't worry, it won't be anything huge, I'm not going to, like, ask you for your kidneys or anything like that."

Robert chuckled, but it sounded a little nervous. "Sure, sounds good."

"All right, just bring the money by anytime this week."

"Actually, I have it now."

There was absolutely no doubt left that this was definitely a good kid. I loved it when customers paid up front. I quickly wrote a note down in my Books that Robert was someone to potentially employ in the future. His size could come in handy at some point.

"Great. Give it to Vince before you leave. And just be ready if I ever need that favor. Thanks, Robert."

"Okay, Mac, thanks," he said, and then squeezed out of the stall.

I sat calmly and waited for the next client, not even suspecting for a second that he would be the biggest problem that had ever stepped into my office.

Chapter 2

Before I tell you about the worst problem I ever faced, I should mention that it was also the worst time ever for it to happen. Because as everybody knows, the bigger a problem is, the more money it costs to solve. And at that moment in time, more than ever before, we needed to make money rather than spend it. We were saving up to go to a baseball game. But not just any baseball game. A Chicago Cubs World Series game.

The Cubs are Vince's and my favorite baseball team in the world. We aren't just normal fans either; we are basically obsessed. We're *real* fanatics, like those crazy European soccer fans. We watch almost every Cubs game on TV and had been planning for years to go to the World Series together if the Cubs ever made it. And we weren't just planning to go to the game like how most people make plans but never actually do them. We were serious. We'd even started a savings account for it, the Game Fund. Well, okay, it wasn't an actual savings account at a bank or anything—it was really just a pile of cash that I kept in my closet. But you get the idea.

Vince and I had been saving for a Chicago Cubs World Series game for the past five years. One game might not seem like a big deal, but it was. The Cubs make the play-offs like once every ten years, and they haven't made it to the World Series in almost seventy years, and haven't won one in over a hundred, which is the longest a single team has sucked in all of sports history. So if we ever got to see a World Series game in person at Wrigley Field, it would be pretty rare. A once-in-a-lifetime chance, basically.

But get this: They are actually good this year. Really good. They are already in the play-offs and are just one win away from sweeping the Dodgers in the first round. I have a feeling that this is the year we'll finally get our chance.

That's why we're trying hard to add as much as possible to the Fund. Getting Cubs World Series tickets will be expensive. Every Cubs fan in the world would want to go to the game, since basically nobody living has *ever* seen a Cubs World Series game before. The tickets would probably have to be purchased through this scalper website because play-off tickets sold out from the real box office in like four minutes flat, so World Series tickets would probably go in under four seconds. They would probably cost at least a couple thousand dollars per ticket, even for nosebleed seats.

We also had to save money to buy the awesome seven-dollar hot dogs, six-dollar sodas, souvenirs, and other stuff like that. Plus we'd need Vince's older brother Victor to take us, which meant we'd have to pay for the gas it would take to drive us there. It's only a few hours away, but gas is pretty expensive. Victor's a cool guy, but he'd never do that kind stuff for free, not even for his little brother.

So it's more important than ever to keep our money flowing in. Like I said, the Cubs are actually really good this year, which is shocking to everybody who knows anything at all about baseball. If everything goes well and they keep winning, their first appearance in a World Series game in almost seventy years is just over two weeks away. We're already so excited that it sometimes feels like pure liquid sugar is being pumped directly into our veins through an IV, like you see in hospitals. I've never looked forward to anything as much as this. Not ever. Not even when my parents took me to Disney World when I was ten.

The problem is that we don't have quite enough money yet. So at that moment every last penny really mattered, making it a horrible time for trouble to just waltz into my office like it did. Well, I guess it didn't so much waltz as it did stumble, but you get the idea.

I heard my last customer of that afternoon shuffle through the bathroom door, his feet reluctantly scraping the floor as if he was being prodded by a stick. I heard Vince pat him down and say, "Hey, kid, you need to relax. No one's gonna hurt you, okay?"

The stall opened and a young kid entered. He was pale with bloodshot eyes. His hands shook as he reached out for the chair. Then he stopped and looked at me. He was asking for permission.

I nodded my head at him and he sat down. He couldn't have been more than a third grader. He looked at the stall's wall to his left, eyeing the ancient graffiti. Middle school cave drawings are how I always think of them. I've spent plenty of time myself looking at the ancient writing. There are classics like "GaRy wuz HeeR" and "Mr JensEN SUX" and "Mitch ♥ JuLie," but there were also a few weird ones like "I WISH I WAS A PEACE OF CHEESE" and "Jason J fly's kites at NitE" and "i eaT what i am."

"What's your name?" I asked, turning my attention back to the customer.

His head snapped toward me as if I had screamed at him. His eyes were big and brimming with tears. He looked like a deer staring into the bright doom of oncoming headlights.

"My name? Oh, it's aah . . . uuh, my name is, umm, Fred."

I studied him for a moment. He squirmed nervously.

"Okay, Fred, what do you need help with?"

"Well, it's uh . . . it's, umm, complicated. He's after me, Mac, and I don't really know where to start, I'm in so much trouble, it's just a mess, it's uh, it's just so . . . oh man, I guess—"

"Fred."

He stopped his chattering the instant I said his name. He looked up at me with his frightened doe eyes. This kid was making me nervous. I don't like being nervous.

"Look, Fred, relax and slow down. I'm having a coronary over here just watching you. Take a deep breath. I can't help you if I don't understand what you are saying. Okay?"

Fred breathed deeply and nodded. He still looked terrified.

"Okay, Fred, let's start with who is after you."

"Staples."

I hoped Fred couldn't see my shock. That couldn't be right.

Staples? Staples wasn't even supposed to exist. The legend of Staples has been spread throughout the town practically since the beginning of time. According to the most often repeated stories, Staples was this kid who dropped out of school after fourth grade and never went back. His age always varied from story to story, but it was generally agreed that he was now between fourteen and twenty. Some kids claimed that he could do forty pull-ups with two seventh graders dangling from each leg. Others said he could pop a tetherball with a single punch. He also supposedly ran a mile in under six minutes and was smarter than Albert Einstein and Hermione Granger combined.

According to the legends, Staples had an intricate web of connections that spread throughout almost every high school, elementary school, and middle school in the city. He was even rumored to have people in the police department. He was untouchable.

They say he used his network to operate an illegal gambling ring. He'd take bets for pro sporting events like football and baseball games, but he mostly took them for local middle school and high school sports games. He also fixed the games. That is, he paid kids to lose on purpose. To miss free throws and easy layups in basketball and fumble the ball in football games and stuff like that.

Some of the rumors even say that Staples is to blame

for the Cubs being terrible for so long. I heard some kid say once that Staples was the one who paid Mark Prior and Kerry Wood to fake injuries their whole careers.

And that was the problem with what Fred was telling me. Staples couldn't be real. No way. I'd never encountered anyone who had actually seen him or claimed to have gambled through his network. And even if he did exist, there's no way his business could have spread here. I would have known about it. I knew everything that happened at this school.

I rubbed my eyes and then addressed Fred.

"*The* Staples?"

Fred nodded and then looked at the floor.

"How can you be so sure?" I asked.

"Because I work for him," Fred said, still looking down. "I used to take bets for him here."

Then he started crying.

I sighed. "Vince?" I said loud enough for my business partner to hear me outside the stall. "You want to join us?"

A few moments later the door opened and Vince stepped in. Fred seemed too busy rubbing his eyes to notice. Normally nobody sat in the stall but me and the customer. But I made exceptions when stuff like this came around. Things as major as the revelation of the existence of a force like Staples. And Vince was the only person I'd ever made that exception for.

Vince gave me a look as he leaned against the stall's wall beside my desk. He must have heard enough from the outside to know what was going on. Vince was the master of giving simple looks that could say a lot.

"I don't gamble myself," Fred finally continued. "I don't even really get how it all works. But there are plenty of kids my age who do. I'd take their money and stuff and then give them their winnings if they ever did win, which was almost never. The legends are true, you know."

"How long has he been operating here?" I asked.

"Umm . . . like three or four weeks or something," Fred said.

"Why now?" Vince asked.

Fred glanced at Vince as if noticing him for the first time.

"He always said that grade schools are tougher to break into because it's hard to find young kids to work for him," Fred said.

"How did you get recruited, then?" I asked.

Fred shook his head. "My brother works for him at the high school in Glyndon. He talked me into it. I was too scared to refuse."

A brief silence followed. The shock of Staples's existence was starting to catch up with me. Especially the shock over how long it had taken me to find out that he really exists.

"Why is Staples after you, Fred?" Vince finally asked.

Fred lowered his head and bit his lip. He looked terrified, as if the very mention of why he's being targeted could get him in trouble.

"Because I tried to leave. I told him I didn't want to take bets anymore and he told me that it was too late. He said nobody quits. And then I said that if he didn't let me quit, I'd tell Principal Dickerson what's been going on around here. And he said that if I did that I would be a rat and rats get the worst punishment of all. He said I would have to eat my food through a straw after they were done with me. I've seen what he does to people, Mac, and I—"

"Hang on, Fred. Why exactly did you want to quit?" I asked.

"Because it's not right, what he does. He's been paying kids to play bad on purpose. Remember last Friday when Kyle dropped that really easy touchdown pass at the end of the game and we lost? Staples paid him to make sure we lost that game. He made a fortune on that one. Lately he's been letting kids make bets even if they don't have money. And . . . and then if they lose their bets, he's been sending the Collector after them to get the money. But the kids don't usually have the money, so instead they've been getting beat up real bad and the Collector steals their iPods and phones and stuff like that. And then they're told that if they ever squeal, then they'll really be in trouble—and one time Staples even threatened to kill this kid's dog. I just can't work for him anymore; the things I seen already . . . they give me nightmares." He was finished, and I could tell that he was fighting back more tears.

"It's okay, Fred. You did the right thing," I said.

That was no way to run a business. I mean, sure, I've had my share of deadbeat customers who never came through on their end of the bargain, whether it be repaying a favor or making full payment. But I'd never rectify it by sending out some hoodlum to rough them up. That just wasn't good business. There were other ways; I had my own method of dealing with welchers, and it had worked just fine this far without ever having to use physical force. In grade school there are bigger things than getting beat up.

"Who is this Collector?" Vince asked.

Fred shook his head. "He's a mean guy. He's an eighth grader, and I think his name is Willis or something like that."

I nodded and rubbed my chin. I knew who Fred was talking about: Barnaby Willis. He was new here; he'd transferred from somewhere out east about a month ago. When I first saw him, I thought he might be trouble simply because of his size and the way he always strutted around like such a tough guy. But so far nobody had complained about him. And I'd heard from other eighth graders that he wasn't much of a troublemaker. Either they'd been too afraid to tell the truth or Willis had been lying low while helping Staples get established. I looked at Vince. We both knew what this meant.

"You need protection, then?" I asked.

"Yeah, I guess, I . . . I didn't know where else to go. My parents would just go to the principal, but I can't let them do that, not now."

"I understand, Fred. I want to help because you seem like a good kid, but I have a pretty strict policy on payment. The only kids who get freebies are the innocent ones. You're not exactly squeaky clean on this whole thing, you understand?" I said.

Fred nodded. I felt bad to take such a hard line. But with the Cubs game just a few weeks away I couldn't afford to just hand out my services for free to every customer who cried. I glanced at Vince. He gave me a slight nod. Like I said before, it seemed like he was more willing to help out kids for no charge. Which was kind of funny, considering he was usually the one stressing about our money flow. But either way it was nice to get his approval to charge Fred for our services.

"So?" I asked Fred after a few moments.

"Well, I still have like twenty dollars left from my last

payday. Is that enough?"

"Sure, that'll be just fine, for a few days at least. This could get pretty dangerous, though, so I may require more later on," I said.

Fred nodded and sniffled.

"It's okay, Fred. We'll protect you."

I leaned back in my chair and looked at Vince again. We both knew this might be bigger than a simple protection job. Had business been slow lately because Staples was cheating my customers out of the money they'd normally be spending on my services? Whatever the reason, I knew I had to focus on trying to protect Fred for now. First things first.

But would I actually be able to protect a defenseless little kid from a monster like Staples?

Chapter 3

"**Y**ou really think it's true?" Vince asked after Fred left. He tossed a baseball in the air and caught it. Vince was always playing around with a baseball. Some of the best ideas we ever came up with happened while we were just tossing the ball back and forth.

I nodded. "Didn't you see this kid? He was terrified."

Vince pondered the situation for a bit longer. "This is a real dilemma. It's like that one time that I wanted barbecue chicken but I couldn't have it because I decided to be a vegetarian for two weeks to see what it was like to be a giraffe."

Joe and I laughed. Vince has this way of making me laugh at the most serious times. It's part of why I love him so much. And the things he says usually don't make much sense because he reads so many books and knows about so much obscure stuff. Nobody usually knows what the heck he's even talking about.

After Fred explained his problem to me, I had Joe post a sign on the bathroom door that said the office was closed for the day. Well, the sign didn't actually say that exactly. It really said, "Caution: Wet Floor," but all the kids know that is code for "closed for the afternoon." If we put up the sign that says "Closed for Plumbing Repairs," then the students know that the office is closed until further notice, which might be several days. I hated closing early. It meant disappointed students and lost money—which was not good for our Game Fund. Right now, though, we needed to think. We sat on folding chairs in the bathroom, eating the lunches that my mom had packed for us. My mom made all three of us lunch almost every day. She always liked to make food for my friends. She was cool like that.

We were supposed to be strategizing, but mostly we chewed and kept saying how much trouble we were in.

Now, you have to understand, I'm not usually afraid of much. I own this school. But if all the rumors about Staples were true, then we were dealing with one dangerous guy. And the last thing I needed was a kid that dangerous to have it in for me before I even had a plan for how to handle him. I needed to think of a way to protect Fred without revealing who was doing it.

"So?" Vince asked. He had been watching me think.

"Let me worry about it. You just make sure that Brady sticks to Fred like gum to the bottom of a desk."

Brady was this third grader who did odd jobs for me sometimes. He happened to be in the same class as Fred, so we decided we were going to pay him a dollar a day to keep an eye on Fred during class and especially in the halls between recesses and lunch.

There are teachers who monitor the halls, but I've found over the years that most teachers are pretty clueless when it comes to how things work among kids. They are never around when the real stuff goes down.

"What about at recess? Who's going to protect Fred then?" Vince asked.

"We'll have to hire more help, right, Mac?" Joe said.

Vince gave him a look. He didn't like the idea of hiring more help because it would be expensive. The more money we spent on this stuff, the less money we'd be able to put into the Game Fund. Vince was always worried about our profit margin.

"He's right, Vince," I said. "We need to hire an older kid to watch over Fred during lunch and recess. We've got to keep the office open, and that's when he'll be most vulnerable. Brady isn't big enough to do it on his own."

"I know we need help, Mac," Vince said as he tossed

me the baseball, "but we'd have to get a seventh grader at least. Do you know how much that will cost us?"

I caught the ball and nodded. He was right, but what else could we do? I felt the stitching and then spread two fingers across the ball like I was going to throw a splitter.

"We may have to dip into the Emergency Fund," I said, throwing the ball back. The Emergency Fund is a pile of money that I started a few years ago. I keep it in my closet right next to the Game Fund, and it's there in case we are ever in a pinch and need a bit of money.

Vince caught the ball and shook his head.

"But that's only supposed to be for *real* emergencies, like if I need an ice cream really bad and I don't have any spare change. Or if I lose a video baseball game because my dumb third baseman makes an error and I get so angry that I throw my whole gaming console right out the window and it smashes the windshield of my mom's car," he said.

I smirked in spite of myself. Even now, when he was genuinely concerned about our money supply, Vince was still joking around.

"If we get to the point where we actually have to use the Emergency Fund, then . . . well, then this whole situation probably *will* be an emergency," I said.

"Actually, I just got an idea for this Fred situation that might help to save some money," Vince said.

That's one reason Vince is such a great business partner—he always comes up with great ways to save money and pinch pennies, thrifty ways to solve tough problems. I mean, sure, his jokes are fun, too, but I'd trade those in any day for his ingenious ideas.

"Let's hear it," I said.

"Well, we could let him hang out in here until we find someone to do it for cheap. That would keep him safe and it would be free," he said.

"Nice, Vince," I said. "But won't that let people know that we're involved?"

"Maybe, but kids are going to find out eventually either way. We'll just make sure we get him here as soon as possible each recess and lunch and hope that too many kids don't notice."

"All right, let's plan to do that for now, but I don't want anything to interfere with normal business long-term. We eventually need to find someone else. We need to keep things running smoothly," I said.

Vince nodded. "It's like my grandma said once. 'When the coin purse is empty, the pocket lint is king,'" he said after a moment of silence.

We all looked at him and then burst out laughing.

Vince's grandma is senile. She is a hundred and three years old or something like that, and she is always saying stuff that doesn't make any sense at all. Most of his family looks at each other uncomfortably when she does that, but Vince loves it. He writes down all the stuff she says in a quote book. Vince loves to quote his grandma. Which I usually find pretty funny.

After a few more minutes of discussion we decided to hire a kid named Tanzeem down the line to look after Fred during lunch and recess long-term, if things went on longer than expected. Tanzeem is a pretty tough seventh grader, and Joe said we could trust him. Joe was going to tell him to meet me here tomorrow during lunch.

This was shaping up to be a pretty tough case, but the one thing I actually thought I had on my side was the element of surprise. Staples didn't know yet that Fred had this kind of protection. Something I learned long ago from watching lots of action movies and playing video games is that having the element of surprise is huge. It's one of the best things to have.

That's why it really sucked that I didn't actually have it. Not at all. We soon found out that Staples somehow knew I was protecting Fred right from the beginning. Kids usually didn't get the drop on me. But then, Staples wasn't your usual kid.

Chapter 4

The first sign that somebody had the drop on us came the next morning before school. I went a little early so I could stop by my office to make a few notes in my Books. I unlocked the door to the bathroom and flicked on the lights, and was in the process of shutting the door so I could lock it when it was pushed back open. The force on the other side was so hard it knocked me backward onto the floor of the bathroom. I sat up and saw the assailant looming over me in the doorway. It was Barnaby Willis, a.k.a. the Collector.

"Hey, look at what I found," he said with a slight accent. He talked like a wiseguy from some New York gangster movie.

He isn't as big as I had thought, but I'm the smallest

sixth grader in the school, so I still didn't stand a chance either way. He wore cargo shorts and a black T-shirt. A small gold cross hung from a neck that supported a pointy face and gelled black hair.

I scooted back and tried to get to my feet but he was too quick. He stepped forward and pressed his foot onto my chest, pinning me to the floor. My lungs felt like a deflating whoopee cushion, only without any laughs.

"No you don't," he said.

I grabbed his foot and tried to lift it, but that only made him press down harder, so I let go.

"So," he said as if he was starting a conversation with an old friend, "I hear that you're harboring a fugitive?"

"I don't know what you're talking about," I said as calmly as I could. It was always best at these times to remain as calm as possible.

"Oh, you don't? Oh, my bad. Sorry about that, sir. I guess I got the wrong guy. Here. I'll help you up," he said, faking like he was going to let me up.

I just lay there, trying to come up with a plan to get out of this.

"Hah! Just kidding," he said, laughing at his stupid joke.

I felt myself starting to panic. Joe or Vince usually didn't stop by here in the mornings. Heck, I usually didn't either. I didn't really stand a chance against this kid by myself and nobody would be coming to help me.

"Do you know that in most states harboring a fugitive is considered as serious an offense as being the fugitive himself?" Willis asked with a playful grin.

"Wow, I didn't know that. Tell me all about it," I said with a mocking air of wonder in my voice.

"Hey! Don't be a smart guy! You're in no position to talk to me like that," he said, pressing his foot down a little harder to make his point.

"Okay," I managed to squeeze out.

"Anyways, like I was saying, your little buddy Fred has threatened to rat out some very important people. Which is a pretty serious offense, as I'm sure you know. And as long as you're helping him, you're in just as much trouble as he is. Understand?" he said.

"Not really," I grunted, even though I understood completely. It was getting hard to breathe under his foot.

He laughed.

"That's too bad, Mac," he said as he leaned in closer.

I saw his fist go back and I braced myself for the blow. I had no idea what to expect because I'd never been punched before. But the blow never came.

The bathroom door opened and then suddenly the pressure on my chest was gone. I sat up and saw Vince standing in the doorway. His mouth was open and he probably looked more scared than I did.

Willis stood up and looked at Vince, seeming nervous for the first time.

"What's going on?" Vince asked.

I almost had to stifle a laugh. That was all Vince could think of to say? He has never been too good at confrontations. But it didn't matter. Vince's mere presence seemed to be enough.

While Willis probably could have taken on both Vince and me in a fight, he didn't even try. He just pushed past Vince and ran out the door. But then, something told me he had been there only to send us a message anyway, and that message had been delivered.

"Are you okay? What happened?" Vince asked.

"I'm fine, thanks to you," I said. "He was just waiting for me, I guess. Jumped me before I could lock the door. He was basically threatening me for helping Fred. What are you doing here anyway?" I asked.

Vince looked at the floor and shrugged. I waited for an actual explanation.

When he realized a shrug wasn't going to be enough, he said, "I was just stopping by to go over our finances."

I nodded. Vince had been spending a little more time at the office than usual lately. He must have been getting pretty nervous about the Cubs possibly making it all the way this year, and us being able to get to a game. I know I was.

"Well, thanks," I said. "I hate to think how that might have ended had you not shown up."

"How did he know that we're helping Fred?" Vince asked.

I shook my head. Though after some thought the answer seemed pretty obvious. If Staples had employees all over the school, one was bound to have seen Fred in line here yesterday and then just put two and two together.

We'd just have to be more careful from now on. Now that Staples knew I was trying to protect Fred, we were all going to be targets. Which meant I really needed to get more information on Staples and his business. I didn't like the idea that he knew more about what I was doing than I did about him. For all we knew, Joe, Vince, and I were the last three kids in the school not working for Staples. The more I learned about this whole mess, the more I realized that it might end up being much more than a simple case of playing bodyguard for a third grader.

That was the first order of business later that day during morning recess: getting as much information as I could on Staples and how his operation worked at my school. I needed to know what we were up against. This was becoming a pretty serious situation, so I reluctantly had Joe hang the "Closed for Plumbing Repairs" sign on the door.

When Fred showed up, Vince went out to take care of some business from earlier in the week and I sent Brady and Joe with him for protection. Vince was pretty big—he was almost half a foot taller and thirty pounds heavier than me—but he wasn't much of a fighter and, as I've said, had never been very good at confrontations. I locked the office after they left and sat down to talk to Fred.

"Okay, Fred, let's start with all the kids you know who work for Staples besides Barnaby," I said.

"I don't remember hardly anybody, and I don't know all their names," he said.

"It's okay, Fred; just tell me what you *can* remember."

"Okay, umm, well, when I saw him, he usually was with like maybe three or four other kids. They're all in high school, except Staples, of course—he doesn't go to school. One of them is his second-in-command or whatever. His name is PJ. He's got short spiky hair and I think he plays hockey and baseball. He's a real jerk, too. He's always making fun of everybody. I don't really know the names of the other ones, but they're all pretty tough. Two of them wear grungy clothes all the time and they have tattoos and stuff like that."

Great. Just great. Staples had a posse of high school

kids and all I had was a few seventh graders if I was lucky. I tried not to let my concern show.

"Go on," I said.

"Well, umm, I only ever met Staples a couple times, but the times I did were at his house. Well, not like inside his house. He has a shed or something that he uses for his office. I don't even know if he's got parents; I mean, his office was pretty dirty. I bet he doesn't got parents."

I nodded. Bad kid with a bad home life. That isn't unusual, at least not according to TV shows I've seen. Getting to a kid outside of the school system was going to be tough, mostly because there were even fewer rules out there.

"Where is his house, Fred?" I asked.

"I don't know. They always blindfolded me until I was inside. I don't think anybody knows where he lives except for those four high school kids."

"Okay, what about here at my school? How does his business work here?" I asked.

"Well, I don't remember a lot of stuff, but I think I heard Staples say once that there were ten bookies including me. We all had our own spots where we went every recess, and then kids came to us to place bets. My spot was by the monkey bars in the grade school playground."

"How many different kids do you think have placed bets so far?"

"I don't know, Mac. Probably like one fourth of all the kids here, but I'm not too sure about that—I'm really bad at fractions. But I do know that Staples almost *always* finds a way to make sure that most kids lose their bets," Fred said proudly, as if that was the most valuable piece of information I could get.

I nodded and smiled at him, but it was obvious that I was already losing control. How could this have been going on without me knowing? Suddenly I felt like I had no power. It felt kind of like when we all went to race go-karts and I had the slowest car. No matter how well I drove, I'd never win because my car just couldn't keep up. I hated that feeling.

"Who are the other bookies, Fred?"

"Okay . . . uh, well, there's Jacky Boy—he's stationed by the merry-go-round—and then there's Andy Aasen and Darren Schmidt, but I don't know where they're stationed, and . . . umm . . . I guess I don't remember any more. I'm sorry, Mac. Jacky Boy was pretty much the only bookie I ever talked to. He was my main contact."

"What about the leader? There has to be somebody in charge here, right? I mean, Staples can't run the whole operation from outside the school, can he?"

"Umm, I don't know. I think Staples does have, like, a top guy here or whatever, but I don't know who it is. It's not the Collector, I know that—he's just muscle. I always just gave my money and bets and stuff to Jacky Boy."

"It's okay, you did good, Fred. Real good." I patted him on the shoulder.

But there was still a lot I needed to learn. First and foremost, I had to find out who Staples's top guy at my school was. Second, I needed to know the identities of all the bookies. The way things were going, it could've been anyone. I didn't like thinking that I couldn't trust my classmates. It was a horrible feeling to have, especially when running a business like mine.

Chapter 5

At lunchtime that day I was supposed to meet with Tanzeem, but he never showed up. After waiting for ten minutes I got concerned and sent Joe to find him and make sure he was okay.

The whole ordeal forced me to close up the office once again, much to the dismay of Vince, and the kids waiting outside the bathroom. In the meantime, Vince, Brady, and I sat in my office and discussed a plan while Fred sat nearby and played his Nintendo DS.

"What do you think?" I asked Vince, who was fiddling with a baseball again. He would always be the first person I asked, and the last person, too, in case he came up with any genius ideas while I was asking everybody else.

"I don't know. I want to get back at that Barnaby Willis guy, though," he said with an edge to his voice that I'd never heard before. He was generally pretty calm, but when people messed with me, he had a real dark side.

"It's okay, Vince. Don't worry about it. We'll deal with that greaseball later. At least we *know* we need to be careful with him. All these other bookies and the guy in charge here are much more dangerous to us right now because we don't even know who they are."

Vince nodded. I turned to Brady.

"Don't you know *any* of the bookies? I mean, kids are placing bets with them, so it's not like their identities are some huge secret, right?" I asked.

"Well, I don't know, Mac. I don't really know any of them myself, and I don't think the kids who *do* know will tell you anyways," he said.

"Geez, way to be positive, Brady," I said.

"Yeah, no kidding. Get out of here with all your smiley faces and bright rainbows and flowers and stuff. You're just choking us with all your corny optimism," Vince said.

"Sorry, guys. I'm just trying to be honest or whatever," Brady said.

"What about Tyrell?" I asked. "We could hire him to find out?"

"No!" Vince practically shouted. It startled Brady and

me a little, and a brief silence followed. "I mean, well, I just don't think he's the right guy for this quite yet, Mac."

I nodded. It figured that Vince would say that. Tyrell is basically my secret weapon in desperate times, but his services are not cheap. Vince rarely likes to call in Tyrell for help. And probably especially right now, business slowing down as it had. Vince had even been spending extra time at the office lately, working his Books even after I'd gone home.

"Okay, we'll hold off on Tyrell for now. I guess maybe that *would* be overkill," I said.

"Yeah, you better just talk to Ears, Mac. He'll know," Vince said. "And at a much cheaper price."

Ears is my main informant. Gossip, fights, detentions, teachers' lounge drama, canceled tests, who is dating who—you name it, Ears has the story. Heck, he could probably even tell you what the principal ate for dinner last night. That's obviously where he got his nickname, because he always hears things other kids don't. That and he also has huge floppy ears.

"Well, let's go find him, then," I said.

Brady stayed behind to watch Fred, but we locked the door just in case. I don't normally like to run errands myself, but with Joe out looking for Tanzeem and my lack of trust in just about everybody outside our business right now, I had no other options.

We stepped out the doors to the lower-grade side of the playground. I squinted in the bright glare of the low morning sun, and after my eyes adjusted to the light, I noticed that almost everyone was looking at us. It's like in the movies when someone does something stupid or some guy walks into a bar or room he shouldn't be in and the music stops and then everyone turns and looks at that guy. That's how I felt just then.

We walked forward a few steps and the kids in front of us all backed away, forming a path. Their mouths hung open and their eyes were the size of hockey pucks. I don't come outside much anymore because I'm usually too busy taking care of business in my office. I almost expected one kid to take off his jacket and lay it out on the ground in front of us so our shoes didn't get dirty.

"Okay, you all need to mind your own business," I said.

After a pause that I thought would last forever, the kids gradually turned away and resumed their games or conversations or whatever they had been doing.

Ears was known to hang around with a gossipy group of girls near the old metal slide. Kids stopped using that slide a while back because it was so slick that chances were you'd crash at the bottom and get a mouth full of gravel. Now, though, everybody stayed away from the slide entirely unless: A) you were a snarky girl with designer clothes; B) you were looking to get ridiculed by said girls; or C) you were a smooth-talking, good-looking guy with an actual chance to date one of the gossipy girls. I'm still not really sure why they tolerate Ears hanging around all the time, because he wasn't all that good-looking or smooth-talking, but they did. There's a lot about girls that I'm sure I'll never understand.

"There he is," I said as we stopped next to the teeter-totters.

Vince nodded.

Ears stood in the middle of the pack of girls as usual. He was talking and they were all listening intently, then suddenly he waved his arms around like he was telling some crazy story, and the girls burst out into snickers and giggles. Ears laughed and pointed at the shoes of one of the girls and said something and they all laughed even more. Except for the girl he pointed at—she just shuffled her feet as if she wanted to bury them into the ground.

"Ready?" I asked.

"Let's do it," Vince said.

As we approached the pack of girls, they turned and stared at us, whispering to each other and giggling. It was a little annoying.

I made eye contact with Ears. When he saw me, his eyes grew to the size of hubcaps. Then he tore away from the slide and went straight down the hill, his shoes skidding on the gravel.

Vince and I looked at each other and took off after him.

We both sprinted down the slope. I almost leaned forward too far and went down face-first into the hard ground, but Vince caught me and held me steady. At the bottom we veered right in pursuit of Ears, who was running across the football field toward the baseball diamond.

Ears had a good head start on us, and neither Vince nor I are track stars, but luckily Ears is pretty uncoordinated and was even slower. I had pulled ahead of Vince slightly and was getting ready to give up because I was so winded. Then Ears tripped and fell.

I pushed my legs just a little harder. Ears climbed back to his feet and kept running for the chain-link fence at the end of the field. I closed the distance quickly and dove for his legs. I wrapped my arms around his knees and he hit the ground hard.

I got up just as Vince got even with us. We lifted Ears to his feet by his jacket.

"Please, Mac, don't hurt me. I'm sorry, Mac," he said.

"What was that all about?" I asked, trying not to yell too harshly. He was still generally a good guy and a frequent employee, after all.

"I don't know, I'm sorry," he said between gasps for air.

I studied him as we all took a few moments to catch our breaths. His ears looked as huge as ever. But other than that, he was a mess. His eyes were droopy and puffy and his hair, tangled and greasy. If he was old enough to grow facial hair, he'd probably have had a mountain-man beard so huge that there'd be birds nested in it.

"What's going on, Ears? You look terrible," I said.

He shook his head and avoided my stare.

"Why didn't you tell me about Staples, Ears? Huh?"

He just looked at his feet.

"You're really in that deep? I don't believe it," I said.

He scratched his neck and grimaced. I could tell he felt horrible.

"Look, Mac, you see, the thing is . . . well, I happen to owe Staples a ton of money and . . . well, he said that he was going to kill my cat, Mac. And I really love little Nevernude. He's the best cat ever, and the only way to get Staples to wipe clean my debt was . . . well . . ."

I sighed.

"Sorry, Mac. I promised Staples I wouldn't help you anymore. I just can't. I knew I never should have placed those bets," he said, and then looked at the sky and shook his head.

"What else, Ears? You wouldn't have run like that just because you agreed not to help me. You're in even deeper, aren't you?" I said.

Ears continued to avoid my stare. After a long pause he finally said, "I'm sorry, Mac. He asked me a bunch of questions about your business."

"What did you tell him?"

"Just basic stuff, I guess. Like who works for you and where your office is, and I can't . . . I shouldn't even be telling you this much, Mac. He'll kill Nevernude! I didn't even want to help him, I swear, but . . . my cat. Haven't you heard about some of the things he's done? I heard a few years ago that he once kidnapped two cops and then made them eat three whole cases of doughnuts and two gallons of coffee and now they both have diabetes and no feet! What would you do if you were me?"

I shook my head. Kids can be so gullible. I mean, I was sure that *some* of the legends about Staples were true, but how could any kid believe that one?

"Whatever, Ears." I said, and nodded at Vince. He released his grip on Ears's jacket and stood next to me.

I shook my head and turned to leave.

"I'm sorry, Mac," I heard Ears call out as we walked away.

I just waved my hand without stopping or looking back.

"We're going to have to find out who the top guy is some other way," I said as we headed back up the hill.

Vince sighed and took out his baseball and tossed it in the air.

"Any ideas?" I asked. "Still sure you don't want to hire Tyrell for this one?"

Vince shook his head. "No, Mac. We just can't be tossing around money like that. I think we should just go after Jacky Boy. If we put a little pressure on him, I bet he'd squeal. He's kind of a little weasel."

I nodded. Jacky Boy was a slimy little kid. But I couldn't complain too much, because he was one of my best sources for getting test answers and copies of homework assignments and stuff like that. At the same time, it didn't surprise me at all that he would become a bookie. That kid would do anything for money. Once he ate a pear covered in barbecue sauce for a dime. He'd probably eat his dog's poop for a fiver.

"I got one for you," Vince said as we reached the top of the hill.

"Now?"

"Sure, why not? Whose numbers are on the flags flying above the left and right field foul poles at Wrigley?" Vince asked.

Vince and I were always challenging each other with Cubs trivia. We each claimed to be the bigger fan, so we were always trying to prove it. The trick was to pop questions at the weirdest times, to catch each other off guard.

The only rule was that you had to know the answer to any question you asked without having to look it up.

"Oh, come on. Billy Williams, Ron Santo, Ryne Sandberg, Greg Maddux, Fergie Jenkins, and Ernie Banks," I said. "I thought you actually had a tough one for me."

"I thought that *was* a tough one," he said with a grin.

Joe was waiting outside my office when we got back. Tanzeem was not with him.

"What happened?" I asked as we went inside. Brady was reading a book and Fred was playing his Nintendo DS.

Then I looked at Joe. He was green, like cartoon characters look when they're sick. I thought he might blow chunks right there in my office. Right in the only stall in the school with no toilet. But he swallowed hard and I was pleased that words came out of his mouth and not his lunch.

"They got to him," he said.

"Who?"

"Must have been some of Staples's guys. Tanzeem got jumped outside of school this morning; they were just waiting for him. I saw him in the nurse's office, Mac, and he was pretty messed up. It was so bad that the nurse sent him home," Joe said.

"Whoa," I said. The school didn't send kids home unless it was really bad.

Joe nodded, looking ill again.

Staples had taken out Tanzeem before I could even talk to him. Which meant that he had known about my plan to hire him. Which led me to believe that Staples possibly had a spy or maybe an informant, or some other way that he was getting information.

"Well, we're just going to have to do this ourselves, then. We'll be Fred's personal bodyguards. He'll just stay here with us every lunch and recess," I said.

I didn't like where this was headed. It almost made me want to go to the principal, but I couldn't. Mr. Dickerson wouldn't get it. He would only make things worse somehow.

Chapter 6

After school that day Joe, Vince, and I walked Fred home. We were two blocks from our school and two from Fred's house, exactly halfway, when they stepped out from behind the shrubs and onto the sidewalk. There were five of them total: Barnaby Willis and four high schoolers.

Two wore baggy clothes and had long hair. They had a dangerous look to them, like they wouldn't think twice before punching a little kid in the face. The other two were athlete types with spiky hair and polo shirts. Barnaby wore the same clothes he had on this morning and also a look of revenge.

Now, Joe is a big guy, the biggest at our school. In fact, he was even bigger than two of the four high school kids in front of us. But he is only an eighth grader, and there is only one of him. We weren't going to be able to fight our way out of this.

"Hey, hey, hey, look what we have here," one of the high schoolers said.

"Yeah, I thought I smelled a rat," said another.

"Oh no," Fred said, tugging at my sleeve. "That's Staples's posse. They do all of his dirtiest work. We're in trouble now, Mac."

I already knew that we were in trouble.

"Who are your new friends, rat?" asked another of the high schoolers.

"Wait, wait . . . I know you. You're that problem-solver guy," said a spiky-haired kid. "It just so happens that I have a problem. Can you help me?"

I just stared at him.

"You see, my problem is that I have a rat and a quitter to deal with, and I don't know how exactly to go about it. On one hand, I could set a trap. I could trick this quitter-rat-snitch and then squish him when he's least expecting it. Or on the other hand, I could just get a stick and take care of this rat problem right out in the open. What do you think, Mr. Problem-Solver Guy? MacGyver, isn't it?"

The other high schoolers laughed at this.

I just kept staring at him. At this point I figured he

must be PJ, the guy Fred had said was second in command to Staples.

"Yeah, that's a tough one, isn't it?" PJ continued. "I guess the best way might just be to pound him into the ground. After all, the more simple a plan is, the less that can go wrong, right?"

He started walking toward us. The other four followed. They walked slowly but with a purpose.

"Split up," I yelled, and grabbed Fred's arm.

Fred and I ran to our right, across the Andersons' front lawn. I didn't see where Joe and Vince went. I pulled at Fred's arm to help him keep up with me. We ran around the side of the house to the backyard. Fred breathed hard, struggling to keep up. I could hear at least two of the five high school kids following us, their heavy footsteps pounding the soft grass. I tried not to think about what would happen when they caught us.

And they *would* catch us. Fred's legs were just too short to outrun high school kids. Not only that, but our backpacks were weighing us down, too. I veered right and headed for the corner of the next house. I pulled Fred along, hoping he wouldn't fall. We turned the corner sharply and then I dropped to the ground, pulling Fred down with me.

I sat with my backpack to the house and listened to our pursuers' approaching footsteps. As soon as I heard them near the corner, I stuck out my leg and held my breath. The one in the lead never saw it coming. I felt a sharp stab of pain in my shin as his feet tangled under my leg and he went sprawling. PJ was running too close behind to stop. He didn't have time to react, and his legs tangled up with the first kid's. They grunted as their bodies collided with the ground in front of us.

I lifted Fred to his feet.

"Run!" I said.

"But, Mac—"

"Fred, just go!" I yelled, and gave him a shove. He took off through the bushes and disappeared behind a fence.

I turned to face my pursuers, who were just getting to their feet. I made sure that I stayed between them and where Fred had run.

"Go get the little rat. I'll deal with this one," PJ said.

The other kid made a move to get by me and I stepped in front of him. He grabbed my shoulders and threw me to the ground and then ran after Fred. I started to get to my feet, but PJ lifted me up first. He slammed me against the house and held me there by the shoulders. The edge of one of my textbooks pressed painfully into my lower back.

"So you think you can get away with tripping me?" PJ said. His breath was hot on my face. It smelled like rotting pizza. I squirmed. "What's the matter? You want to get away?"

"Yeah, your breath smells. Don't you ever brush your teeth?" I said.

"Whoa, look at that. You're just a little punk, aren't you? Staples is going to have a lot of fun with you," he said. "But not before I do first."

"We'll see," I said.

"I was going to go easy on you but not anymore," he said, still pinning me to the side of the house.

I was just starting to formulate a plan when I saw Fred come out of nowhere. He ran right up behind PJ with his backpack reared back to strike. I instinctively flinched as Fred started swinging it toward PJ.

The next thing I knew I was on my feet and PJ was on the ground holding his side.

"Come on," I said, and grabbed Fred's arm.

We ran back toward the alley. My shin and back ached and I wanted to stop, but I forced myself to keep going. I led us around the next house and across the street. We crouched behind a bush.

I peeked back through the leaves.

PJ stood up and grabbed his ribs. He bent over and it looked like he was trying to catch his breath. Then after a few moments, he calmly walked toward the street, away from where we hid.

PJ met up with the kid who'd chased Fred after I'd tripped them. The kid shook his head and raised his palms to the sky. PJ shoved him and said something harshly. The other kid shook his head again. Then they walked down the street and out of view.

"How did you get away?" I asked as we remained hidden in the bushes.

"I just hid and he ran right by me. He's kind of dumb," Fred said.

"Thanks, Fred. You really saved me."

Fred just shrugged, but I thought I saw him blush.

We waited in the bushes to make sure the coast was clear. My shin and back still ached. I felt pretty helpless. That was twice in one day that I had been cornered and then rescued. I didn't know whether to feel lucky I had good friends or ashamed that I couldn't defend myself.

After I was convinced that Staples's posse was really gone, we headed toward Fred's house. I dropped him off, making sure he was safely inside, and then I jogged to Joe's backyard.

We had agreed long ago to meet there if we were ever split up unexpectedly. Vince's trailer park was the farthest away, near this neighborhood called the Creek. It was the dirtiest, shadiest neighborhood in town and everybody knew that that's where you went if you needed drugs or something like that. Pretty much everybody stayed away from the Creek unless they lived there. And my house wasn't a good option because that's where we hid the Funds. In a time of panic or danger why would we want to lead anyone there?

When I got to his house, I found Joe sitting calmly on the stump of a tree that had been cut down a few years ago. Joe had convinced his dad not to dig up the stump and it became Joe's favorite chair. He always called dibs on it long before Vince or I could even open our mouths.

"Hey, Mac," he said.

I nodded at him. It looked like he'd put up a good fight. He had a reddish purple eye and his lower lip was a little swollen.

"You okay?" I asked.

"Oh yeah, fine. I'm kind of worried about Vince, though," he said.

Joe was one tough guy, that was for sure. I didn't think I would be so calm after getting punched in the face. I didn't think any kid could be so calm after getting punched. It's moments like this that make me pretty happy he's on my side.

"What happened to Vince?" I asked.

Vince was a funny guy, and he was super smart and good with money and numbers, but like I said before, he's not very good at confrontations. He usually just avoids them altogether. Joe caught his breath while I looked out into the street. I didn't see any sign of Vince. Joe's house was only a few blocks from where it had all happened, so Vince should have been there by now.

"What happened, Joe?" I asked again, trying not to sound as panicked as I felt.

"Well, the other three came right after me first and Vince ran. I think Barnaby wanted revenge, because basically the two high schoolers held me down while Barnaby pounded me like a punching bag. But then Vince came back. He shouted at them to get their attention and then he started making fun of them. He really let them have it, too. It was pretty funny. Anyways, one of the high schoolers went after Vince and that's the last I saw of him. But he saved my butt, because once it was down to just two, I was able to fend them off pretty easily. After I got a few punches in, the chickens took off just like Willis did this morning," Joe finished. That sounded like Vince; he was basically the least glamorous hero that ever existed.

"We should go look for him," I said.

"I'm sure he's okay, Mac. He had a decent head start."

I nodded. And we needed to wait there because that's our protocol if we get split up in a pinch. But it wasn't as easy as it sounds. Just sitting there while Vince was possibly in danger was basically torture.

We waited for almost ten minutes, but it seemed like ten days. I was starting to get so worried that I thought I might cry, which would have been embarrassing. I kept picturing the horrible things those high school kids might've been doing to Vince right at that very moment. All the while Vince would probably be trying to make jokes, too.

Finally, Vince showed up. He came walking casually into the backyard from the street. He looked okay, as far as I could tell.

"What took you?" I asked. Though, really, I didn't care. I was just relieved he'd made it back in one piece.

"I just wanted to make sure it was all clear. Are you okay?" he asked.

I nodded.

"Thanks for helping me out, Vince," Joe said.

"What happened? Didn't he get you?" I asked Vince.

He shook his head and laughed.

"It was close, but I got away. When he came after me, I ran faster than I ever have before. He chased me all the way down to Pete's house. He was going to catch me, too, but I knew that if I got to Pete's house his mom would be outside gardening. And I knew that he wouldn't dare touch me with some lady watching."

Pete's mom was obsessed with her garden. One time we were over at his house playing baseball in the street and the ball landed in her garden. She screamed at us and then picked the ball up and threw it on the roof. She was kind of crazy.

"So she was outside, then?" I asked.

"Is the Pope Catholic?"

"I don't know, is he?"

"Yeah. My grandma always says the Pope is Gouda, but I think that's a cheese and not a religion," Vince said while grinning. "Did you get Fred home okay?"

"Yeah, the little kid actually saved me."

"You were saved by a third grader," Joe said.

Vince laughed.

"Whatever," I said. "What matters is that this is bigger than just Fred now. We're in for a fight. A dirty one."

Joe and Vince nodded.

This was nowhere close to being worth twenty bucks. But I had a reputation to uphold. And Fred needed my help. He had saved me back there. Not many third graders would have had the courage to do that.

Tomorrow we had to start thinking about ourselves. We would get revenge for what they had done to Joe and for the attack this morning. We obviously had more to worry about than just protecting Fred now. Or even just protecting ourselves. The whole school was at risk. Staples was dangerous, and he wasn't going to just shut down his operation on his own.

Besides, what else did I expect? I couldn't just keep protecting Fred forever. Eventually I'd run out of money. Eventually more kids would come to me for help with Staples. We couldn't live like this. The only way to end this was to get Staples out of my school for good. We definitely needed to do more than simply protect Fred; we needed to take down Staples.

Chapter 7

I guess that this is as good a time as any to take a moment and tell you about how our business got started. How Vince and I built it up out of nothing.

It all started when my family lived in this trailer park called Bella Vista. I was in kindergarten and we had just moved to town. Vince lived in the trailer next to mine. He was really nice to me right from the start, which was cool because nobody likes being the new kid.

The day we moved in, my parents were moving boxes inside and unpacking and stuff like that. I sat out in the grass in front of my trailer playing with some Transformers.

"Hey," I heard someone say.

I looked up and saw a kid about my age standing

over me. He had dark hair and dark eyes and he was smiling.

"Hi," I said.

"Is that Soundwave?" he asked, nodding at my Transformer.

"Yeah," I said.

"Cool. He's my favorite. Hey, do you like nachos?" he asked.

"Uh, yeah, why?" I asked.

I was pretty sure that he was going to ask me to come over and have some with him because that's usually what followed a question like that, but of course at that time I didn't know what Vince was like.

"Cool. Me, too. Hey, do you want to go play football?" he asked.

"Uh, okay, sure," I said.

After I got my parents' permission, we set out walking toward the huge playground across the street. I saw some kids of all ages in a clearing running around and throwing a mini football. I'd never played with older kids before, so I was already really nervous. At that time I didn't realize that that's just how trailer parks are. They're kind of like their own little club. There were only so many kids living in Bella Vista trailer park, so they all usually kind of hung out and played together regardless of how old they were.

"My name's Vince," he said as we walked toward the clearing.

"Cool. I'm Christian."

Right before we got there he said, "Have you ever seen a rattlesnake in real life before?"

"No, have you?" I asked, hoping that he had and that he'd tell me all about it.

"Nope," he said, and then he didn't say anything else.

After a while longer he said, "My grandma says that pudding is the only reason to get out of bed in the morning."

I started laughing and so did he. I knew it already—I was going to love hanging out with this kid. He'd made me laugh even though I was so nervous I felt like crying.

When we got to the playground, Vince coughed loudly and said, "This is Christian. He's a good friend of mine and he wants to play, too."

"Okay," said an older kid holding the football. "I'm Barry and this here is Eric." He pointed to another older kid. "We kind of run the football games here. You're totally welcome to play if you want."

"Thanks," I managed to say. I was still nervous, but these kids seemed pretty nice. And it was Vince who had gotten me the invite.

"Hi," said a few of the other kids closer to my age.

Then we played football. Well, we played football

as well as a group of kids between kindergarten and fourth grade could, which was with lots of fumbles and dropped passes and not a lot of rules, even though we still spent a lot of the time arguing over the few rules we did have. But it was fun, mostly because I'd just made a new friend.

Vince came over the next day and we played video games. And the following day I went to his place. Pretty soon, we were hanging out every day. And I still hadn't got tired of Vince saying stuff like, "My grandma says that the only real way to eat a pinecone is with tortoise gravy and a sense of self-worth."

We would go over to each other's trailer and play video games and board games. We used to do this thing called Gameday. It was where we would play all of the board games we owned on the same day. And we would track our scores and keep records of who was winning and losing in this huge notebook. That was Vince's idea. Turned out he was obsessed with statistics and records even back then. It's no surprise he eventually became the business manager.

The point is: We were pretty inseparable. And one of our favorite things to do was to bring all of our action figures to this huge playground in the middle of the trailer park and play desert action movies and stuff. We did this almost every single day during that summer between kindergarten and first grade.

But one day we got there and found the sandbox occupied.

Some kid sat in it playing with a Tonka truck. He wore a black cape and his dark hair was all slicked back tightly like a smear of oil.

"Hey, this is our spot," I said.

The caped kid looked up; his face was cool and calm.

"Noch tchoday hittsch shoht," he sloshed, spit spraying from his mouth.

"What?" Vince asked.

The kid held up his index finger and then reached into his mouth and removed a set of white vampire teeth.

"I saaaaaid, not tooodaay it's not," he replied, and smiled a dark and evil grin.

"Look, we've been coming here every day for forever, so you should move. You can go play in the sand under the swings," I said, pointing over the kid's shoulder. "It's big enough for you to play in, but it's not big enough for us. That's fair, right?"

The kid continued to smile and said, "Kristoff, the Dark One, moves for no mortal."

"Well, it's two against one, and we'll beat you up, so you should just move, okay?" I said. I didn't really like making threats, but we just wanted to play. Even an immortal vampire was no match for the two of us and I think he knew it.

"Yer gonna pay for this," Kristoff said as he got to his feet. He shoved the teeth back into his mouth, tucked his truck under an arm, grabbed the edges of his cape, and ran toward a white trailer across the street. He flapped the cape continuously the whole way home.

We sat down in the sand and began to play. About twenty minutes later I spotted Kristoff making his way back into the park. And this time he had someone else with him.

"Uh-oh, look who's back," I said.

Vince turned and watched Kristoff and an older kid slowly make their way over to the sandbox. They stopped about ten feet from the edge of the sand. A huge smile was planted on Kristoff's face. The older kid was maybe a third or fourth grader. When you're in kindergarten, a third or fourth grader can be pretty intimidating.

"Who's that?" I asked.

"This is my brother, Mike," Kristoff said.

We looked at Mike. He wore jeans and a T-shirt. He didn't really look that mean or scary. But he was big and he was scowling at us.

"I heard you little punks have been giving my brother a hard time," Mike said.

"Oh no, he totally started it. He took our spot," I said.

"Well, that's not what he says, so how about you guys

move so he can play in that there sandbox?"

Vince and I looked at each other. We shrugged.

"Well, we're playing right now," I said.

"See, they're jerks!" Kristoff squealed.

Mike nodded.

"You can play over there," I said, pointing at the swing set sand.

"Noooo, he's going to play right there in that sandbox and you're going to move," Mike said.

"You gonna make us?" Vince asked defiantly.

Instead of answering, Mike started walking toward us. I hadn't been all that scared up to that point, but suddenly as this older kid approached looking more and more like a giant, it began to seem possible that Vince and I might soon find our faces forcibly buried in sand.

When Mike was just a few feet away, I said, "It's two against one, you know."

He responded by reaching out for my shirt, and as I tried to back away, my feet tangled and I fell onto my butt in the sand. Then the terror took over. You need to remember that we were just kindergartners. And the world is pretty different when you're that young. It may have been two against one, but as a fourth grader, he was basically twice our size. And he seemed a lot tougher than both Vince and I put together.

We screamed, grabbed whatever toys we could

manage, and ran as fast as we could toward my trailer. Mike and Kristoff ran after us. Which led to some more screaming and running on our part.

I heard them behind us. I wasn't sure how close they got or how hard they were actually trying to catch us, but I wasn't about to try and find out. I just kept on running. Eventually we made it to my trailer. I turned around and saw Mike and Kristoff standing across the street, on the edge of the playground. They laughed.

Then Kristoff yelled, "This is our playground now, so don't ever come back!"

We went inside my trailer, feeling pretty dejected.

"Oh man, that was close!" I said. "Are you okay?"

Vince nodded. "Yeah."

"Do you think they'll be gone tomorrow?" I asked.

"Yeah. I bet they were just showing off," Vince said.

But the next day Mike and Kristoff were still there. And the following day Mike and Kristoff were there yet again. And the next day as well. Pretty soon, we came across other kids who Mike and Kristoff wouldn't let into the playground either. Mike and Kristoff had taken it over.

The only times any of us ever got to go in the playground that summer were when we were either with our parents or Mike and Kristoff were inside eating dinner or something. But those times weren't very often, and we wanted our playground back.

That's when we devised a plan. It was officially the first of many plans that Vince and I would develop together.

One afternoon we went to the edge of the playground and peeked around the corner of a nearby trailer. There they were: Kristoff, the Dark One, and his older brother, Mike. They were swinging side by side on the swing set.

It was time for phase one. We went back to my trailer and found my dad in the living room watching TV.

"Hey, Dad?" I said.

"Yeah?"

"Will you come play football with us in the play-ground?" I asked.

"Can it wait until after *Quantum Leap*? It's over in about ten minutes."

I knew he'd say that. He watched reruns of this old, weird TV show about a time traveler and a computer named Ziggy every day in the summer from three to four. He never missed an episode and it was almost impossible to get him away from the TV while it was on. My mom had given up trying years ago.

So far, the plan was working perfectly.

"Okay, we'll go get the football and then meet you there?" I asked.

"Yeah, okay."

"Thanks, Dad!" I said, and we left my trailer.

We walked back to the playground slowly. We needed the timing of the plan to be perfect, so we couldn't rush it.

"Wow, your dad really loves that show, huh?" Vince said.

"I guess."

"Yeah, my mom loves this show called *Doctor Who*. It freaks me out," he said.

We reached the edge of the playground once again. Mike and Kristoff were still swinging. It was time for phase two of the plan. We walked boldly out into the middle of the playground and stopped just behind the swing set.

"Hey, freak! Want to come suck our blood?" I yelled.

Mike and Kristoff dismounted immediately and turned to face us. The two of us stood staring at the two of them as the sun beat down on the thirty feet or so in between.

"What're you doing here? This is our playground now!" Kristoff yelled.

"We just want to play in our sandbox like we used to," I said.

"No way. That's our sandbox now," Mike said.

I looked back across the street toward my trailer. I saw my dad just leaving the front door. I took a few steps toward the vampire and his older brother.

"Well, we're here now, so we're going to play in the sandbox," I said.

Mike started walking toward me and said, "You really want to do this?"

"Go ahead, make my day," I said. I saw some really cool dude say that in this movie I watched with my dad once. It was kind of boring, except for the part at the end where he says that line to this guy and then blows him away with a gun the size of Texas.

Mike kept moving toward me and I held my ground, just hoping that the plan would work. If not, I'd be in trouble. Mike stopped just a few feet away. He squinted an eye at me, as if to make sure I was still there and wasn't an illusion. Then he scowled and reached out a hand faster than my eyes could move. He grabbed my shirt collar and pulled me up and toward him. His other hand formed a fist and I closed my eyes, waiting for the blow.

But then everything went still as a deep rumble fell down from the sky like the voice of an angry god.

"HEY! *What is going on here?*" my dad thundered as he walked into the playground.

Okay, I should explain something. I know it's pretty wussy to hide behind your daddy, but we were just little kids and Mike was practically a giant gorilla or yeti or something compared to us. Besides, the smartest and best plans were usually the ones that involved cheap shots. Like in a fight, if you really want to win it, then you'll bite and scratch and kick people in the groin instead of just punching and wrestling "like a man."

"You let him go, *right now*!" my dad said.

Mike let go of me and backed away. His and Kristoff's faces turned white as Elmer's glue. They looked terrified. And I didn't blame them. My dad, well, he's pretty big and scary. He's a football coach, so he has lots of experience at yelling and screaming. When he yells, he yells pretty loud and his face gets real red and his huge neck bulges with veins. He's like six feet ten inches tall and weighs almost four hundred pounds, pure muscle. He'd scare anybody. But not me, because I know he is a pretty cool guy.

"How dare you threaten my boy? What are you thinking? You're twice his size!"

Mike and Kristoff both looked at the ground. Mike shrugged and Kristoff started crying. They looked pretty scared and ashamed.

"I don't *ever* want to see you out here acting like that again! You got that? Because I'll call your parents! Who are you, picking on little kids half your size? What are you trying to prove?" my dad finished.

Mike put his head down and trudged back to his trailer. Kristoff followed. Kids' faces poked around trailers, trying to see what all the commotion was about.

They smiled when they realized what was happening. The playground was free territory once again.

"Next time idiots like that are harassing you, come tell me," my dad said to us. "Now, are we going to play football or what?"

My dad's pretty cool. That was the only time I ever involved him in any of my plans. I like to keep my family out of my business and my business out of my family. It's worked well that way so far.

Anyways, word quickly spread throughout the trailer park that I had been behind the ingenious plan to get rid of Kristoff and Mike. Those two still played in the playground occasionally, but they mostly kept to themselves. In fact, sometimes we even let Kristoff play action figures with us in the sandbox. Turned out, he was an okay kid.

But back to the point: Everyone heard that it was me who got rid of them. It was my dad not me who scared them off, but Vince was going around telling everybody he came across, "Christian did it; he saved the playground. Hey! Hey, want to know who solved all our problems? Well, I'll tell you: It was Christian. My best friend and super genius."

We both knew he was exaggerating a little and he thought it was pretty funny. But deep down I knew that he meant most of it, too. I always tried to tell people that

Vince had helped a lot. That it had been Vince's idea to somehow use my dad in the plan. But he'd always try to hide from the attention and make sure that it came back on me. It's been like that ever since; Vince is always building me up and staying out of the spotlight himself. He is so good at it that it can even get a little annoying sometimes. It's like he built me up so high that a lot of people don't even know who he is at all. But in the end, I think it's simply enough for him to know that *I* know how much he did for the business. He just didn't ever want the glory.

Anyways, pretty soon after the whole showdown Vince started telling kids that I could help them with other problems, too. And eventually the other kids *did* start coming to me for help, and somehow I was able to solve their problems.

I honestly don't know what it was. I just always had a way of knowing what to do for every kid's situation. I mean, it wasn't rocket science; back then the problems were really easy. It was stuff like loaning out a video game or helping to organize a lemonade stand and stuff like that. I guess they just didn't know how to do that kind of stuff on their own.

It was also Vince's idea to start charging fees for my services. I was a little unsure.

"Isn't that kind of mean, Vince? I mean, these kids

don't have hardly anything," I said.

"I know, Christian, but listen. You're helping them in a major way. They'd be lost without your help. So why not get something in exchange? They're being helped, and we're getting payment. Both sides gain something; everybody wins," he said.

"Yeah, I guess . . ." I started.

"Christian, think of it this way: It's kind of like at the fair when you order a funnel cake and it's all warm and greasy and covered in powdered sugar, and oh man, it's so good. And then you eat it all and lick the sugar and grease off your fingers and it's just delicious."

"What? How is it like that at all?" I said.

"It's not. I just really want a funnel cake right now," he said, rubbing his stomach.

"Okay, okay. It's a pretty good idea," I said, trying to hold back a laugh, "but how will they pay us? I don't know many kids who have more than like fifty cents, and a lot of them are coming to *me* for money to rent a game or something like that."

"Well, they can like let us borrow some of their video games. Or maybe they can owe us a certain amount of their Halloween or Easter candy. Or maybe sometimes they could just owe us a favor of some sort. They don't always have to pay with money."

"You know what, Vince? I think you're the real genius

here," I said, and I meant it, too.

I think he knew I was going to say something like that, because as I said it, he crossed one single eye and scratched his head, and he had this blank look on his face. Then he got up and started chasing around a butterfly while giggling like a madman.

So I eventually agreed that it was okay to charge kids for my services. Besides, how many first graders do you know who make their own money without any help from their parents? Exactly.

That's pretty much how the business got started. We made my first office in the sandbox of that trailer park playground.

We kept running the business there until eventually my family moved into a house in a different neighborhood. Vince still lived in that same trailer, and actually still does now, but the distance from my new house made it a tough place to run the business from, which is why we finally decided to take our operation inside the school. In part it was because as time went on, the neighborhood near that playground got more dangerous, so it wasn't really safe to be hanging out there by ourselves all the time. But Vince also had the genius idea of tapping into kids' school problems, because as we got older, we realized that school started to take up more and more of kids' lives.

After we moved into the school, the problems got more complicated, which led to larger payments. Pretty soon, we had an operation that brought in more money than we knew what to do with. We were unstoppable. And it was because it was a team effort, right from the beginning, with his ingenious business ideas and my problem-solving skills.

That's why it seemed so significant that a little kid like Fred could have a problem so huge that it was threatening the very existence of our business.

Chapter **8**

The morning after Staples's posse ambushed us went pretty smoothly. Especially considering it was day one of our war against Staples. We ran the business like usual during early recess. The only difference was that Fred sat in the corner of the bathroom where we could keep an eye on him. He was supposed to look at the customers and let me know if any of them were on Staples's payroll, but mostly he just played his Nintendo DS.

Thankfully, most of the morning customers had easy problems, like wanting me to get them McDonald's for lunch or other stuff like that. There was one customer, though, whose problem concerned me a little bit.

It was this fourth grader named Matt Murphy. He

was known for picking his nose and eating his boogers in class. He'd try to hide the act by leaning over and huddling down near his desk, but that didn't really hide anything from the kids sitting in front of him. He was pretty well known as an "eater," and he was generally considered to be pretty gross by all the girls. I always thought he seemed like a good kid, though, despite his bad habit.

"What's your problem, Matt?" I asked as he sat down.

"I'm, well, I've been told that you could help me with anything, anything at all, right?"

"Of course, as long as it doesn't involve, like, killing a raccoon and then barbecuing it in the alley behind your house or something like that," I said.

He smiled but it was humorless.

"I made some bets and lost and I don't have the money to pay for them. And now I'm going to be collected, Mac!"

"You need a loan, then?" I asked.

"Well, maybe . . . I don't know," he said as he leaned over to play with his shoelaces.

"What do you mean you don't know? How much do you owe?"

"Uh, like a hundred and fifty dollars," he said.

This was the part where, if I'd been drinking something, I'd have sprayed it all over the desk. But I wasn't, so instead I just gawked at him.

"I know, I know," he said. "It's just that Jacky Boy, my bookie, kept saying, 'Double or nothing, Matt, it's the only way. Come on, Matt; don't be stupid, you'll never pay it all back. You have no choice, really. Double or nothing, Matt,' and on and on like that. I—I just never realized how high it had gotten."

"I see," I said as I regained my composure.

He was screwed. Flat-out. I had that kind of money, but I'd probably have to dip into the Emergency Fund. Which I wasn't about to do for this kid. But I did have another solution in mind and it would help me on two fronts.

"Do you know who they're sending after you?" I asked.

"The Collector, of course," he said. "And he's bad news, Mac. He already collected my friend Evan. The Collector hurt Evan's hand pretty bad, and stole his bike and made him tell his parents that he lost it! How do you convince your parents that you *lost* a bike?"

I shook my head.

That settled it. Barnaby Willis would be the first to go. Evan had been on my baseball team the previous summer. He was a good kid and a really great short-stop. Anybody who would do something like that to Evan deserved to be taken out. If the assault on me yesterday morning and the beating he laid on Joe after school weren't enough, this certainly was. Plus, taking out Willis seemed to be the natural first step to bringing down Staples. Hopefully kids would be willing to talk once he was out of the picture.

"Okay, here's the deal. I'm going to buy you a little time. I'm not saying how I'll do this, but just know you'll be safe for a little longer. So you'd better start saving up some cash. Come back to me in a week or so and show me what you have and I'll try to loan you the rest, okay?"

"Okay, Mac, thanks," Matt said, looking relieved. He left the office as the bell rang.

So that was that. I needed to take out the Collector, a.k.a. Barnaby Willis. And I knew just where to go for help.

At lunchtime we closed up the office. And then we made the East Wing boys' bathroom the most dangerous place in the school. The playground probably threw a party that day.

Nine visitors stood near the sinks. They watched me warily, but also with a hunger that I found pretty unpleasant. We were normally enemies, most of these nine and I. But not today.

I stood in front of nine of the school's meanest, most dangerous and vile bullies, jerks, punks, and tough kids.

Never before had our school witnessed such a large gathering of bullies as it did on this particular Wednesday. Usually it would have been hard to get these sort of kids to meet me here, but we managed to convince them by offering ten bucks each. Even the most vicious of bullies can be tamed with money. It was an expensive meeting—ninety bucks to be exact—so I hoped that it would pay off in the end.

Vince especially had been annoyed at the cost. I wasn't sure what was with him. He was always a little concerned over our expenditures, but lately he's been freaking out over every penny. I swear, I wouldn't be surprised to see him out on the streets selling his school lunches to homeless guys for an extra buck. But I guess it probably has something to do with the Cubs being closer to the World Series than ever in our lifetimes.

I normally liked to stay out of the bullies' business unless a customer made it my business. Bullies are part of the social order of school and it wasn't my place to mess with that. I may not have liked it, but in the end I never could have stopped all of the bullies all of the time anyways. To be honest, our business depended on the bullies a little, like an exterminator depends on rats and bugs. But now I was meddling in the bullies' business because I needed their help. I needed mercenaries. I needed muscle.

I looked at the group of kids in front of me; each of them could beat me senseless in one way or another in less than a second. Which is why I also had Brady join us that day, for some extra security. There were seven boys and just two girls, each more dangerous than the last. Maybe I should stop here for a moment to tell you a little more about the bullies, so you can get an idea of what I was dealing with.

1. Nubby—Nubby kind of sticks out because he is by far the biggest of the bunch. He is a seventh grader and the kind of bully who picks on other kids to avoid being bullied himself. I guess he really buys into that whole "best defense is a good offense" sort of thing that coaches are always talking about. Nubby is kind of fat and has a lot of freckles and his left hand has only stubs of fingers, due to some unknown accident. That's why people call him Nubby, because of his stubby fingers. Rumor is he lost the fingers in a horrible petting zoo mishap, but nobody seems to know for sure if that is actually true.

Nubby is definitely an easy target for teasing, but he happens to be bigger than the other kids. So instead of being nice and getting picked on, he's mean and quick to club kids over the head with his fingerless mallet of a hand anytime they even look at him funny. Nubby really isn't too bad of a guy, though. Whenever kids come to me for help because Nubby is bullying them, it's usually pretty easy to get Nubby to lay off. A bag of chips, some candy, that sort of thing.

2. Little Paul—Little Paul, or LP as some kids like to call him, is actually pretty little. I know in lame movies the huge guy is always nicknamed Tiny and the little guy is always nicknamed Jumbo. But this is real life and not one of those stupid movies. In real life kids usually just call it how it is.

Not that Little Paul can really help being little—he is only a second grader, after all. But that doesn't mean the kid still doesn't have a real mean streak. He's confident and talks a big game, and he never backs down from a fight, no matter how outmatched he is. But the truth is that no second grader can take Little Paul by himself. He is the master of the first strike. The kid always strikes first and strikes hard. At least seven independent eyewitnesses once reported that with a single blow he dropped a hundred-and-fifty-pound sixth grader like a sack of potatoes.

The general rule with LP is: If you get on his bad side, you'd better have your head on a swivel, because he can come out of nowhere and take you down before you even know he's there.

3. Snapper—Snapper looks pretty harmless, if you're one of those people who consider little third-grade girls harmless. But everybody at my school knows better. Snapper is one of those girls who is used to getting her way; she is a brat through and through. Which in itself isn't all that bad. But it is triply terrifying considering that her signature move is a bite so hard it would snap a man clean in half if her mouth were big enough. And it isn't too far off. Sometimes if you look at her right before she's about to strike, her face is all mouth and nothing else.

Lots of little girls are biters. That's not really all that new. But the difference with Snapper is that she is an especially talented biter. If she isn't getting her way, she strikes fast and hard. Once her iron jaws are clamped around whatever appendage you're unlucky enough to have too close, you can pretty much kiss it good-bye until either several teachers are able to pry open her jaws or she simply gets tired of making you beg for mercy.

The worst part about Snapper's bite and perhaps what makes it especially deadly is that struggling only makes her bite harder. One kid even was poking her in the eyes and pulling her hair so hard we all thought she would soon be bald, but all that did was make her bite so hard that she broke the skin and the kid ended up with an infected arm for three months.

4. The Hutt—The Hutt got his name because he kind of looks and sounds like Jabba the Hutt from the *Star Wars* movies. He has thick lips and a slimy, sluglike appearance. He also slurs his speech, and when he does talk, it is with a raspy, gurgling voice. And I bet he would choose to ride around on a concrete slab with Princess Leia chained to him if that was possible. He is kind of a slobby, gross kid, and normally that would make him ripe to get bullied himself, but the fact is that the Hutt is a jerk, flat-out. He is an eighth-grade bruiser and often likes to trip kids in the halls for no reason other than to show everybody else just how cool he thinks he is. The sad truth is that Jar Jar Binks is more likely to ever end up with a girlfriend than this kid, and that makes me feel a little bad for him, despite the fact that he's usually nothing more than a mean blob of slime.

5. Kevin—Kevin is your typical, run-of-the-mill, good old seventh-grade bully. He's tall, big, has a lot of freckles, and likes to make kids miserable. His standard move is also pretty classic: He's a lunch-money guy. He thrives on lunch money the way zombies thrive on brains. It got so bad at one point that the school had to lower the prices on their à la carte items, such as cookies, pizza, and Little Debbie snacks, because so few kids could afford to buy that stuff anymore. Oddly enough, that was the one year that our school actually passed the Presidential Physical Fitness standards in gym class.

A lot of kids come to me for help with Kevin and I do what I can. But sometimes it seems like there are at least *twenty* Kevins running around the school feasting on kids' lunch money. One day, a day that everybody now calls the Day the Lunch Money Died, Kevin had thirty-three confirmed attacks spanning six different grade levels. It had been the largest-scale lunch money massacre in history. There's no question that Kevin has a hunger for lunch money that goes far beyond basic greed. I was eventually able to get Kevin to lay off the younger kids for the most part, which is better than nothing. Plus, he's gotten so good at taking lunch money that he rarely has to beat anybody up anymore. Kids basically just throw their quarters at his feet as he walks by them in the halls.

6. iBully—iBully is a tall fifth grader who weighs about sixty pounds, pure skin and bone. He's pale and his hair is oily and there have been only seven or eight confirmed sightings of him outside in the fresh air in school history. But that doesn't mean he can't still inflict a serious amount of damage.

iBully is a computer bully. He is the master when it

comes to hacking kids' email and Facebook accounts and wreaking havoc on their personal lives. He logs in and sends nasty emails to your best friends. He writes inappropriate messages on teachers' blogs and Facebook walls and Twitter accounts. He even once sent a horrible message to the President of the United States from this one kid's email account, and these dudes in black suits showed up in dark SUVs with tinted windows and escorted the kid out of the school. The kid came back three days later and he hasn't spoken a word since. Not one.

iBully is part of the reason that I never made a Facebook or Twitter account for myself. It's just too dangerous, with him constantly lurking in the neon-glowing depths of the computer lab. Well, that, and I also think Facebook and Twitter are pretty lame. I always preferred, you know, talking to people face-to-face in real life instead of stalking them online like a creeper.

7. Great White—Great White is a shark, just like his name might make you think. But really people call him Great White because he has super pale skin, white hair, and freaky whitish blue eyes. He's a tall and lanky seventh grader, and he's British, too. Normally, most kids would probably laugh at the weird way he sometimes talks, using phrases like "give it a go" and calling the

·86·

TV a "telly" and saying "maths" instead of "math." But laughing at his weird British accent would pretty much be the last mistake any kid made.

According to Ears, Great White moved to America because he was kicked out of darn near all the schools in England. I'm not sure if that's true, but it definitely seems possible. I don't know how things work in Britain, but Great White is a real scrapper. He is probably the best fighter at our school. Some kids say they've seen him take out four eighth graders at one time. He also isn't easy to buy off. When kids need help with Great White, one of the only ways to stop him is to send this bully named Kitten after him. I'll get to Kitten in a bit.

8. PrepSchool—PrepSchool isn't your ordinary bully. In fact, I don't think she ever punched, hit, slapped, or physically harmed another person in her life. Her bullying is more of the mental variety. She has an ear for gossip and a knack for filling in the pieces that she doesn't hear for herself. And she isn't afraid to talk either.

Some nerdy kid in my gym class did a study once, and he calculated that something like 93.9 percent of rumors started within the past two years originated with PrepSchool. His study was pretty scientific, too—he even had charts and graphs and stuff called probability differentials and mean ranges that made this one kid get a nosebleed during the presentation because it was all so technical.

PrepSchool seemingly picks on any kid she wants. She's only a sixth grader like me, but that still doesn't stop her from targeting anybody and everybody. Prep-School turned the most popular eighth grader in the whole school into a weirdo loner who now wears a painted burlap sack to school—by starting one simple rumor that the girl's dad is a birthday clown for hire. We later found out this is true, but still.

PrepSchool got her name because she's always going on and on about how she is going to go to this private girls' preparatory school in Connecticut instead of the public high school up the street and that she was going to get so much smarter than all of us and go to Yale University and become some big-shot Corporate Suit with three pink sports cars and a dog named Snuggles. A lot of girls are pretty jealous of her and I guess that's probably why everybody believes what she says about the other kids all the time.

9. Kitten—Kitten is by far the king of the bullies at our school. Actually, he is the king of everybody. No one messes with Kitten, not even me. But he doesn't cause a lot of problems either. I have to hire Kitten a lot to keep total control over the other bullies. If one of them ever gets too tough or mean, then I just send out Kitten. I actually wanted Kitten to be my permanent strongman, but he wasn't really into being constantly ordered around in public and who was I to argue? In the end I'm glad Joe ended up getting the job, but sometimes I wonder what could have been. Either way, the point is that Kitten and I are usually on the same side. Thankfully.

Kitten got his nickname because he looks like a kitten. Not really, like with fur and stuff, but you know, metaphorically or whatever. He has a real nice look to him, with neat, short, and perfectly parted hair. And he always wears sweaters and collared shirts and he has big kind eyes. Plus, he's really little and meek, one of the smallest sixth graders in the school. His voice is real high and soft, like he might start crying at any moment. He looks and acts like the biggest mama's boy in the whole state.

How can he be the top bully?

Kitten is a psychopath, pure and simple. He looks like an angel, but if you get on his bad side, he'll go nuts. He uses weapons and teeth and fingernails. One time in math class he did something with a compass that would get most people arrested. Another time he wrote all over some guy's brand-new white basketball shoes with a black Magic Marker. He's crazy and everybody knows it, so they leave him alone and listen to what he says. The thing about Kitten, and part of the reason I like him so much, is that he only bullies if someone else starts it. He never picks on innocent kids for no reason. He isn't a mean guy. Just insane.

All of the bullies grouped around me in the East Wing bathroom were pretty dangerous. I had a good mix, and presently they all looked a little cranky. They wanted to know why I had dragged them from their lunches to be here. Apparently, ten dollars only got me so far. I decided I'd better start talking.

"I bet you're all wondering why you're here," I said.

A few of them nodded and Great White scoffed.

"You're all here because I need your help," I continued. "It seems that someone has invaded my territory. No, *our* territory. His name is Staples."

I paused for the reaction.

The younger ones gasped. I think a few of the older bullies didn't believe me. They thought, like I once had, that Staples didn't exist. But a couple bullies looked calm or almost embarrassed. It was possible that they owed Staples money already.

"It's true," I continued. "I didn't believe it myself, but he *is* here and I need your help to get him out of our school."

"Why? Why should we help you?" Great White said. His British accent made him sound tough and cool.

"First, he's cheating you guys. He's fixing all the local sports. Some of you may have debts already and you're probably going to end up paying for them with a broken arm or maybe your iPod or bike. If you help me, your debt will be gone. Second, if Staples keeps recruiting kids here and takes over the school, there aren't going to be bullies anymore. At least not independent ones like you guys. The only bullies will be his cronies and bookies and the Collector. Would you like that? To lose control?" I asked. "Third, I will pay you."

"How much money are we talking?" Great White asked above the murmur of the other bullies.

"Twenty dollars for each task completed," I said.

I saw Vince flinch and clench his fists. I knew he would hate that; it would set us back at least another few days in saving up for the upcoming Cubs game, which was possibly just a few weeks away. And paying the bullies that much would basically drain our entire savings and force us to dip into the Emergency Fund. But the future of our whole operation was on the line. Why didn't he see that?

A hush came over the bullies. That was pretty good money, considering they bullied for simple lunch money as it was now.

"What sort of tasks?" Kevin asked.

"*Fun* ones," I said, and smiled. "The kind that will allow you to be yourselves."

Great White let a sharky grin spread over his gaunt face. I saw some of the other bullies perk up, too, except for Kitten. His face looked blank, which wasn't surprising. Kitten always looked composed and rarely talked.

"Let's get one thing straight now," Great White said. "I'm doing this for the money, not to help out you blokes. I'd just as soon hoover my baby sister's spilled shreddies every morning or skip holiday this year."

I tried not to laugh. I saw some of the bullies biting their cheeks, doing the same thing. It was always hard not to laugh at the way Great White talked. Apparently British people called vacuuming "hoovering," cereal "shreddies," and vacations "holidays." England must be one weird place.

"That's just fine," I said. "Tell yourself whatever you need to, just remember that if we don't take down Staples now, then you run the risk of going from the bullies to the bullied."

"You think some kid is just going to come in here and start pushing us around because of some stupid gambling thing? Pfft, whatever," the Hutt slurred. He wasn't the only one who seemed unconvinced.

"Look, you can believe me or not. If you want the

truth, I don't really care either way what you think. Let's just say that you're right and that Staples never will be a threat to you guys. If that's true, then what have you got to lose by helping me? Nothing. All you have to do is a few odd jobs and you'll be much richer for it. I'm basically making charity cases out of all of you; why in the heck would any of you turn me down? Are you scared or what?"

"Are you calling me a chicken?" Little Paul asked. His little fist was balled up, and he took a step forward.

I took a small step back, wary of his first-strike capabilities.

"No, of course not," I said. "Not if you're willing to help me out. But if you *are* too chicken to help, believe me, I totally understand. I mean, who could blame you, right?"

Several bullies shuffled their feet and I saw most of them glancing around at one another to see who might be the first to show fear, which is the ultimate sign of weakness for a bully. One flash of vulnerability with everybody watching and their status as school bully could come crashing down in the blink of an eye.

After nobody spoke for a few more seconds, I finally said, "Good. It's nice to see that none of you are too scared or stupid to turn down such a lucrative offer."

"What's our first, like, task or whatever?" Nubby asked.

"The first task is the elimination of Barnaby Willis, otherwise known as the Collector. I want him taken out. Immediately."

"Just, like, go beat him up or what?" Kevin asked.

"It's more than that. I want him to be completely convinced that it's in his best interest to stop collecting kids. Permanently. I'm ordering a hit on him. In movies that usually means killing the guy or dumping him into the river or something. Obviously I don't want that. I just want him to stop collecting debts. Understand?" I said.

The bullies looked at me with blank stares. I sighed.

"Look, I want *you to collect him*. Take his stuff. Do whatever you have to do—just make him know what it feels like to be collected. Make Barnaby Willis wish that he never came to school today."

Again, I just got more blank stares in response. I guess that's why these kids are bullies and not honor students.

"Okay, look, meet up with me at the start of late recess and I'll tell you exactly what to do, all right?"

"What about me?" PrepSchool asked, her arms crossed and her hip jutting out like she had better places to be. "What am I supposed to do? I'm not getting involved in any fighting, okay? I can't risk losing my acceptance into Hanover Academy, plus I just got a mani, if you couldn't tell."

I hid a smirk. "No, you can start by spreading a rumor about the Collector that causes kids to laugh at him instead of fear him."

"Hey, I don't deal in rumors, okay? What do you take me for? I'm not like some lame gossip girl. I don't have time for that kids' stuff."

I looked her right in the eyes until she looked away. "Well, I guess there's no reason for you to be here, then, is there? I guess that saves me some money, too. You can go now."

She didn't move. "Wait. You said twenty dollars for each task if I go along with this stupid thing, right?"

I nodded.

"Fine." She sighed as she shifted her weight so that her other hip was now pointing at me like some sort of huge accusatory finger.

"Same with you, iBully. Your job is to try and destroy Barnaby's street cred by breaking into whatever personal online account you can find for him."

iBully wheezed and nodded while his fingers flickered rapidly across a touch-screen phone he'd been fiddling with the whole time. Knowing him, he'd probably been hacking into Canada's Homeland Security database just while we'd been talking.

I smiled. "All right. I'll see the rest of you at the start

of late recess, then. Except for Kitten. I need you to stick around for a minute. I've got a special assignment for you."

The rest of the bullies started leaving. As Brady ushered them out of the bathroom, I looked at their eager faces while trying to ignore the sudden feeling that I was letting loose a bunch of wolves into a flock of lambs.

Soon only Kitten was left. He looked at me, waiting for his special assignment. Now that a plan to take out the Collector was in place, it was time to move to phase two.

"Kitten," I said, leading him toward the fourth stall, "how would you feel about *convincing* somebody to come in for a meeting with me?"

His face remained expressionless, except possibly for the barest hint of a smirk.

"I thought so," I said, and then proceeded to tell him exactly what I had in mind.

Chapter 9

Later that lunch period Joe ushered in a small weasel-like kid. He looked terrified and it was obvious why. Kitten was standing right behind him.

Kitten's special assignment had been to bring in Jacky Boy for a "meeting." I figured that all of Staples's employees here had probably been warned not to talk to me, so I knew he'd need a little convincing. I sent Kitten instead of Joe, because Joe's method of persuasion would have been physical force, and the recess supervisor probably would have noticed a huge eighth grader dragging a little kid across the playground against his will. I figured that Kitten would be able to get Jacky Boy here much more subtly. And it appeared that I was right.

Vince searched Jacky Boy and his backpack for

weapons or recording devices.

Kitten stood behind them looking calm and bored, as always.

"Thanks, Kitten," I said.

Kitten shrugged and slipped something he'd been holding into the pocket of his khaki Dockers dress pants and then left the bathroom. I didn't even want to know what he'd used to "convince" Jacky Boy to come here. I'd learned long ago not to even ask Kitten about his methods. I slept easier that way.

It had been Vince's idea to bring in Jacky Boy for "questioning." He'd come up with it the night before while we watched baseball together. As valuable as Joe was to our business, our best ideas usually came up when it was just me, Vince, and a Cubs game. It hadn't actually been a Cubs game last night, but baseball is baseball.

I led Jacky Boy into my office and pushed him into the chair across from my desk. Then I sat down myself. I folded my hands in front of me and looked at my visitor. Jacky Boy was a fourth grader. He was a little money-grubbing ferret. But he had provided my customers with test answers and homework answers and forged progress reports and other stuff like that many times. So, while I didn't really like the kid, it would be best for future business dealings if I could get the information I needed without using threats.

"Jacky Boy," I said, nodding my head in a greeting.

"Why am I here, Mac? Why did you send that psycho after me?" he said. His high-pitched whine of a voice pierced the quiet of the small stall like a cactus needle stabbing your ankle. "I've got work to do."

"I know, Jacky. It's just that I've got work to do, too. And my work and your work are sort of related, so I thought we could help each other," I said.

"I don't know what you're talking about, Mac."

I shook my head and sighed.

"Jacky, Jacky, Jacky Boy. Do you really think I'm that stupid? Are trying to offend me?" I asked as sincerely as I could.

"No, Mac, it's not that. It's just—"

"Jacky Boy. You're working for Staples for the money, right? Well, I can help you make even more money. And you can keep on working and taking bets. I'm not asking you to quit. So why are you playing dumb? Don't you want more money?"

He eyed me suspiciously with his beady black eyes. He licked his lips and I saw a line of sweat trickle down the side of his face.

"What do you want?" he asked, sounding like I might ask him to eat a school lunch or something crazy like that.

"All I want is to talk to your boss at this school. You see, I'd like to partner up with him; I want to help him run things better here. I know he usually hangs out on the middle school side, but I don't know exactly how to contact him. Can you help me?" I asked.

Obviously I had no idea where his boss hung out; I didn't even know who it was. But I wanted Jacky Boy to think that I *did* know who it was. I knew that it must be a middle school kid, because Fred had made it clear that Staples didn't trust little kids very much. There's no way his top guy here would be younger than seventh grade.

"How will that make me more money?" he asked.

"Jacky Boy, a better-run business usually means more money for everybody involved. Know what I mean?" I said. Then I moved a piece of paper off my desk, revealing two crisp ten-dollar bills underneath.

I swear when he saw the money, his face lightened as if the sun was shining right through the roof, spotlighting him like he was in a play. His mouth foamed with spit, and his beady eyes got just a little bit wider and brighter.

"All I have to do is help you meet up with Justin?" he asked.

Justin. Now I had a first name. I went through all of the Justins I knew who were older than sixth grade. I could eliminate several right away because they were either too stupid to ever be given that kind of job or they were straight-A students who were so well-behaved that they asked for the teacher's permission just to breathe.

I narrowed it down to two: Justin Johnston and Justin Slauter. Slauter was a possibility, but he was really into sports and he was *so* competitive that one time after he missed a free throw in gym class, he desecrated a basketball and then threw it at some kid on his own team. So it didn't seem likely that he would get involved in a business that dealt with losing on purpose. Justin Johnston, however, made perfect sense.

"Yes, that's right, Jacky Boy. I just want to meet up with Justin Johnston. I'll contact you later with a time and place, okay?" I watched for a reaction.

He nodded calmly. He did not correct me or make any reaction. So Staples's head guy here *was* Justin Johnston. That didn't surprise me. He's a real jerk. I don't like him. I think he's no good. I never really worried too much about Justin, though, because despite his being one mean seventh grader, Joe is bigger and stronger. But now with Staples at his back Justin was much more dangerous. It was no wonder that nobody had complained about him in a while. He'd been too busy running a dirty gambling ring right under my nose.

I slid the twenty dollars across the desk. Jacky Boy pounced on it. I thought he was going to stuff it in his mouth and eat it, the way he grabbed it. But he just stuffed it into his pocket and got up to leave.

"One more thing, Jacky," I said.

He sat back down. Now he looked intently at me. He wanted more money, so I had his complete attention.

"I want to place a small bet."

I slid another ten across the table. He put his hand on it and then took out a small notebook with the other.

"I put ten bucks on our eighth-grade football team making the regional tournament this year," I said. It was as sure a thing as I could think of. Our school's football team had never, ever missed the regional tournament in the fifty-plus years of being a school.

Jacky Boy nodded and wrote something down. He put the ten dollars in a small compartment in his backpack.

"I'd like to bet with each bookie . . . kind of as a peace offering. But I don't know where they're all at. Can you tell me where I can find them all, so I can place some more bets?" I said.

He told me the names and locations of the other nine bookies operating at my school.

I thanked him and he left. Vince came in, and I let a huge smile spread across my face. Just like that we had the name of every kid in the school currently working for Staples. We also had the identity of his top guy here, Justin Johnston. Now that I knew exactly who I was up against, I could start making an actual plan to take them all out.

"We're making progress," I said to Vince. "We might

have this whole thing cleared up before the World Series after all."

"Yeah, but we probably won't have any money left," Vince said.

I rolled my eyes. "Yeah, that was expensive, but you can't deny the advantage it just gave us. Now we know who we're gunning for. We're not fighting blind anymore."

Vince nodded. "You're right. That was a pretty nice move, Mac. Man, that Jacky Boy kid sure loves money. He treats money like my grandma treats the Pintsized Midnight Moonbeam Workers who live in her purse."

I laughed and it echoed throughout the bathroom. Vince's grandma was always opening her purse and talking to the Pintsized Midnight Moonbeam Workers. Sometimes she'd just say hi, but other times she would thank them for all the money they left in her wallet.

"Those darn Moonbeam Workers. I need to find out how to get some of them to live inside my wallet," Vince said.

Later that day Joe, Brady, and I stood on the edge of the upper-grade playground and watched as Kitten approached the recess supervisor. We could see every inch of the playground from our carefully chosen spot.

Kitten tugged at the edge of the RS's shirt. She turned around and smiled when she saw who it was. Adults adored Kitten as if he was the greatest thing since the advent of manners. Adults just went crazy over the whole dress pants, nice hair, sweaters, and dress shirts thing. Plus, he used "please" and "thank you" more than any kid I knew, and those words were like drugs to adults.

We watched as Kitten started talking to her. He pointed at something down near the goalpost of the football field. Then he grabbed her hand and led her away. She was happy to follow, of course. Kitten didn't talk much normally, but, man, could he tell long and pointless stories like a pro when he needed to. And for some reason adults always found his stories really cute and interesting.

As soon as I was sure that Kitten had the RS's complete attention for the duration of his story, I turned my hand over and passed a small mirror under the sun's light. I saw it reflect brightly across the playground to where Vince was waiting for my signal.

He nodded in our direction and gave his own signal to Little Paul. Except Vince's signal was a massive sneeze so obnoxiously loud and overdone that I thought I'd blow the whole operation by laughing myself to death.

Little Paul heard the signal and then approached Barnaby Willis, who was playing basketball with some seventh and eighth graders. Little Paul walked right into the middle of their game. He was one brave little kid, that was for sure. They all stopped and watched as he walked up to the kid with the ball, took it from his hands, and marched right up to Willis. Willis towered over him by at least a few feet. But that didn't stop Little Paul for a second.

What he did next actually went a little above and beyond what I'd instructed him to do, but it still worked. He threw the ball right at the Collector's face. It bounced off the Collector's nose with a rubber *pop* that sounded like he'd just bricked it off the rim. Everybody on this side of the playground gasped.

Then Little Paul took off running. Willis followed just like we knew he would. A guy like the Collector doesn't let a little kid get away with disrespecting him in public.

Little Paul was a fast kid and he easily stayed ahead of Willis as he ran toward the portables. The portables are these three small buildings that the school built to house specialty classes. Like for the kids who are LD or MR or ADHD or ADD or JLCA or GKD or TNIF or whatever other letters adults label kids with.

Behind the portables is the official fighting rink. Everybody knows that if you're going to fight somebody, you take it behind the portables. The portables have no windows and the recess supervisor never goes back there. Plus, with the portables all side-by-side, there is enough room for a whole crowd of kids to watch without being seen. The spot has been used so many times that a large circle of trampled dirt has replaced the nice green grass.

Little Paul led the Collector around to the back of the portables. As soon as he cleared the end portable, Vince gave the other bullies their signal. They descended upon Willis like a pack of starving monkeys at a flea market. What happened next was pretty hard to watch, in all honesty. Willis was a crying mess by the end, and to add insult to injury the bullies even stole his wallet and shoes. After finally prying Snapper off his ankle, the bullies told Willis that if he ever collected one more kid, they'd collect him twice as hard next time.

I made eye contact with Vince during the aftermath. I could tell he was thinking the same thing I was: What have we done? I'd be lying if I didn't admit that the whole thing made me feel horrible for the rest of the day, even in spite of what the Collector had tried to do to me on Tuesday.

But what mattered was that the Collector was out of commission, which meant it was now time to fix the problem at the source: getting kids to stop placing bets. If we cut off the supply of gamblers, then the money would stop coming in. If the money stopped flowing, then Staples's business at my school would collapse. Easy as pie. Or as Vince's grandma sometimes said: Easy as dressing up like a tree to catch wombats.

Chapter 10

After school that day I found a surprise in my locker. Not a good one, though. I opened my locker to put away some books and get my Cubs hat. And there it was, staring at me with the type of vacant look that only death can supply: a dead rat.

I was just barely able to hold back a yell. I think probably the only reason I didn't make a fool of myself right then and there was because the rat lying on the top shelf of my locker was actually pretty small and white, like the kind that are in the school science lab, and not a huge gray beast like you see in movies that eats small deer for snacks and would give you the bubonic plague.

After I reminded myself that it was really just a mouse after all, I nudged it onto a piece of paper and tossed it in the garbage. Although the dead rat had been gross, that wasn't what was bothering me. It was the message it was supposed to send. I looked around inside my locker and found the note I knew would be there.

I unfolded the piece of paper; on it was a simple message, handwritten: *Friends of rats end up dead. Give us Fred by the end of tomorrow or you'll be roadkill!* Vince showed up just as I finished reading the note.

"What's that?" he asked.

"It's nothing," I said as I tossed the note into my locker and slammed it shut. I decided not to tell anybody—they'd just panic. The last thing I needed was Joe and Vince panicking. Besides, there was no way I was going to just hand over Fred. Not now. We were way past that.

"Oh," Vince said.

"What? No joke?"

He shrugged. "Nah, I'm not really in the mood for jokes."

Something was up. Vince was almost always in the mood for jokes. The longest he ever went without making a joke was after his dad died. That was about four years ago. For two weeks afterward he and I just hung out in the old trailer park playground. We didn't really do much—we just sat on the swings next to each other and I pretended not to notice that Vince was crying. I don't think he was ever embarrassed about it. I think he was just happy to have me there and that was good enough for me.

I remember feeling helpless. Here I was the kid who had the answer to everybody's problems, but I had no answer for Vince. There was no trick I could pull off that would bring my best friend's dad back. I'd have given up anything, but it just wasn't possible. Eventually Vince had sort of found a way to move on. But it still bothers me to this day that I hadn't been able to do more for him when he needed it most.

"What's wrong, Vince?" I asked.

"Oh, nothing, just a bad day at school," he said.

I nodded, but I wasn't sure I believed him. He's too smart to have bad days at school. In fact, I'm pretty sure he's smarter than every teacher he's had. But I let it go. Everybody was allowed to be in a bad mood once in a while.

"Say, I'm going to head to the office after school to go over some numbers, so you guys can head out without me. I'll still see you tonight, though, for the game," Vince said.

"Sure thing," I said. Vince had never spent much time at the office alone before. I was starting to get a little concerned. I guess the Cubs actually being good was affecting him more than I'd thought.

• • •

That night Vince and Joe came over to hang out and discuss some regular business matters. Joe left when Vince and I switched the TV to the Cubs game at seven.

"Baseball is so boring. How can you stand to watch it all the time?" Joe said as he got up to leave.

"What?" I said. "Not if you know what you're watching, it isn't. Baseball is the thinking person's sport."

"Plus, I mean, it's the *Cubs*," said Vince.

He looked at Joe with concern. Like a doctor might look at a patient with a massive head injury. Joe laughed and called us crazy one more time before leaving.

"All right, Vince, I've got a good one for you," I said as the first inning got underway.

"Give me your best shot, Trivia Master," Vince said sarcastically.

It was a relief to see that humorous glow back in his eyes. I guess whatever he'd done back at the office after school had cheered him up.

"Okay, then, in nineteen thirty which Cub had one of the greatest offensive seasons in baseball history with fifty-six homers and *one hundred ninety-one* RBI?"

"Whew, that is a tough one . . . but, uh, you'll have to do a little better next time, Mac. The answer is Hack Wilson."

"Whatever, you cheater," I said.

"Right, how can I cheat at trivia? I can't help it if my brain just happens to hold more Cubs knowledge because I'm a bigger fan than you."

I grinned and threw a handful of popcorn at him.

After a few minutes Vince's face got really serious.

"What is it, Vince?"

"Mac, you *do* realize that we're not going to be able to afford to go to the game at this rate, right?" Vince said.

"What do you mean?"

"Mac! You just promised those bullies almost two hundred dollars for beating up Willis. That's a lot of cash, my friend. We don't really have the money for pay-outs like that." He sounded as worried as I'd heard him in years. And maybe even a little angry.

"We'll be okay. Don't worry, once we get this Staples thing taken care of, then we'll just work extra hard to make up for it," I said.

If Vince was telling me we wouldn't have enough, then that was probably true. Vince was almost never wrong when it came to money. Then again, he was also overly cautious when it came to our finances.

"Do we *really* have to pay everybody so much? They probably would have worked for less," Vince said.

"Yeah, okay. I'll try to be more careful. Sorry."

"I just think I'd snap if the Cubs make it this year and we miss out on the game. Plus, it's not like these kids need our money all that bad. These are bullies, Mac. They steal other kids' lunch money. I just think that if we're going to blow our chance to go to a Cubs World Series game then it should be for a better cause."

"Jeez, Vince, I said I was sorry, okay? Don't you think I know that? I'm just doing what I think is necessary to save our business. Do you have a better idea?" I kind of regretted my tone as soon as the words left my mouth. This was getting too close to a fight for me.

"No, I guess not. I just think sometimes you forget what it's like to not have everything you want all the time," Vince said.

"What's that supposed to mean?" I asked.

"Nothing, forget it," Vince said.

I hesitated. Had he been referring to the fact that my dad is still around? Or that my family moved out of the trailer park and lives in a house now? If so, where the heck did that come from? He knows that everything I have is his, too. We share everything.

"This is just the worst time ever for Staples to suddenly show up," I finally said.

Vince agreed with a nod and we left it at that. We rarely argued about money, but the Cubs game was changing things a bit.

The Cubs won that night, advancing to the National League Championship Series for the first time in over ten years. They just needed to win four of their next seven games and they'd make it to the World Series for the first time in basically forever. The good news was that they'd dominated their next opponent, the Phillies, all season long; the bad news was that the tickets weren't getting any cheaper. We needed extra money now more than ever before.

After the game Vince and I looked at each other and nodded. We didn't even have to say it. Going to this game was truly a once-in-a-lifetime opportunity, and we couldn't let it pass. We *really* needed to take out Staples, and fast.

The next morning (which was Thursday, in case you're keeping track), we all gathered in the bathroom at first recess. Me, Vince, Joe, Fred, Brady, and the nine newly hired bullies. The bathroom got kind of hot and smelly with that many kids all grouped in there. We tried to ignore the smell as I congratulated them on their successful hit. Barnaby Willis hadn't even shown up to school that day. PrepSchool said word was he had to transfer to a new school due to some of the absurdly vulgar emails iBully had sent to the school board from Barnaby Willis's email account, but coming from her, I had no idea if I could believe that.

I gave them their well-earned twenty dollars and

then started discussing phase two of the plan to take down Staples's operation at my school.

I went over the names of all the bookies that I had discovered as well as where they were normally stationed. I showed the bullies school photos from the year before and gave them instructions to patrol the area around their assigned bookie, making sure that no kid got near enough to place another bet. If the kids still tried to get by, then the bullies were supposed to convince them that it was not a good idea.

"What do you mean convince them?" Nubby asked. "Like with words or what?"

"Make them not want to place another bet," I said.

"How do we do that?" Nubby asked.

"By whatever means necessary, if you know what I mean. Make them an offer they can't refuse," I said. I heard someone say that in a movie once. It's one of my favorite phrases.

"What do you mean by that?" Great White snapped. "Stop talking in bloody riddles and just tell us what to do, aye!"

"Intimidate them, use a little bit of force if you have to, just get them to stop placing bets. Only don't go overboard; I don't want any of these kids to have to go to the nurse, okay? These kids are *not* to be roughed up like what you did to the Collector."

With that I assigned them each a bookie and gave them ten bucks.

"I'll be out monitoring the situation this afternoon and if I'm satisfied with the results, you'll get the other ten dollars," I said.

Then they left to go wreak havoc on my school. I felt a little nauseous. I didn't really like paying nine of the meaner, tougher kids at the school to go intimidate and bully mostly innocent kids and cause problems. But for the sake of our business, the future of the school, and the Cubs game, it had to be done.

At lunch that day we closed up the office so Joe and I could go monitor the progress of our plan while Vince stayed behind to watch over Fred. We started out in the upper-grade playground. Everything appeared to be going well. The bookies stood at their stations alone. Every time a potential customer approached, the bully assigned to that bookie would get in their face and the customer would sulk away. Pretty soon it became obvious to the kids on the playground what was happening. After a while nobody even tried to place a bet, especially after Snapper almost bit off this one kid's thumb to keep him from approaching the bookie.

It was when Joe and I were on the grade school side of the playground that I saw something shocking. We had just finished watching some kids make fun of one of the bookies about this really horrible rumor that PrepSchool had started about him sneaking home chunks of the school meatloaf in his backpack because he was building a meatloaf castle in his bedroom that he was going to live in with his pet hamster, Charleston.

Anyways, we moved on to Jacky Boy's post and that's when I saw him. I didn't know who it was at first because his back was turned to us, but some kid was having a heated conversation with Jacky Boy. Jacky Boy kept slamming his finger into his palm as if he was expecting the kid to put a stack of cash into it. The other kid shook his head so vigorously I thought it might fall off and roll down the hill, where someone might mistake it for a kickball and punt it out into the street.

Joe and I glanced at each other and repositioned ourselves so we could get a better look at the kid Jacky Boy was arguing with. The recognition hit me like a medicine ball chest pass from Arnold Schwarzenegger.

It was Brady.

I motioned for Joe to go check it out in person while I considered the implications.

But before I even really had a chance to process what it all might mean, the attack happened. I should have been expecting it, considering what we had done to Barnaby the day before, but I guess I didn't realize just how many kids Staples had under his control.

Right after Joe left my side, I felt hands grab my shoulders and spin me around.

"I've been looking for you."

I looked up at the kid's face. It was a pretty big seventh grader who I recognized but didn't really know.

"What?"

"Did you really think you'd get away with all this?" he said.

"With what?"

He looked confused. I tried to look confused back.

"You're Mac, right?"

"Who?" I said, making sure I looked more lost than ever.

His grip on my shirt loosened as he tried to figure out if I was lying. I quickly pulled away from him and ran. I headed toward the teeter-totters. I could feel him right behind me.

I heard kids cheering me on as if it was some sort of game. I wanted to yell at them to trip the kid instead of just yelling stuff like, "Yeah, go, Mac!"

I quickly hopped onto an empty teeter-totter and ran to the middle so it tilted down the other way. My attacker ran around to the other side and stopped. He smiled at me. I stood in the middle of the teeter-totter, balancing it so it was parallel with the ground.

"Let's go, loser. You trying to get me or what?" I said to my attacker.

He scowled and charged at me.

As soon as he lunged forward, I jumped from the middle of the teeter-totter onto the seat behind me. The other end fired up like a Chuck Norris roundhouse. I didn't actually see what happened, because I was too busy making sure I landed on my feet, but I heard a crack that sounded like a baseball being crushed out of its skin by a wooden baseball bat.

The attacker was on the ground moaning and I felt a little bad. I stepped toward him to see how badly he was hurt, but he looked up like he was going to murder me. I turned to run as he started getting to his feet, but there was no need. Kitten just came flying out of nowhere and did what he did best: something insane.

He was bent over my attacker, and while I couldn't see what was happening, the screams coming from the seventh grader were horrifying. "Aaaah! Okay, okay, please!" the seventh grader pleaded.

Kitten stood up, a stapler hanging from his hand in the open position. The kid's pants leg was full of staples.

I helped the seventh grader to his feet.

"Let's go," I said, and led him around to the side of

the building where I could talk to him privately. Kitten stayed close.

"Are you done?" I asked the kid as I shoved him against the school.

"Yes, yes. I'm sorry. I only did that because I owe Staples a lot of money and Justin said that I wouldn't have to pay him back if I beat you up. He said something about avenging Willis or something like that, I don't know . . . I hardly know the guy."

"How did you know to find me out here?"

"This is just where Justin told me to watch out for you. That's all I know, I swear. I didn't even want to do it, but I had no choice." His eyes nervously flickered back and forth between the stapler in Kitten's hand and my face.

I nodded and took a step back. The kid pulled at the places on his leg where Kitten had stapled him and then whimpered like a puppy.

"Okay. I'm going to let you go. But I better not ever see you in this sort of situation again. Got it?"

"Yeah. I swear, I really didn't even want to do it in the first place. Thanks, Mac, really," he said, and then limped toward the school. I watched as he went inside, probably to the bathroom, where he could cry in privacy.

Justin had known that I was going to be out here

today. And I'd had no idea to even watch out for that kid. Something definitely wasn't right. First the Tanzeem thing and now this. I was getting a bad feeling that I had a snitch on my hands, and considering what I saw just moments before the attack, I had a good idea of who it might be. One thing was definitely pretty clear: I couldn't really trust anybody outside our business anymore.

During afternoon recess I dismissed all of the bullies and my other employees except for Fred, Joe, and Vince. There was no sense in moving forward with any further plans until we took care of the snitch. As long as Staples had a man on the inside, none of us were safe. I scheduled a meeting for Joe, Vince, and me for later that night to discuss what to do about the mole.

At least the plan to neutralize Staples's influence here was working for the time being. No bets were being placed and we had eliminated the Collector. That's why it was too bad that it all came crashing down after school that day. A day I now refer to as Black Thursday.

Chapter 11

That day after school as Vince, Joe, and I walked Fred home, I heard someone shouting for help. It was coming from an alley that ran behind the houses across from the school. There were actually a few voices yelling for help.

"Hear that?" I asked as I veered off toward the alley.

"Yeah, Mac, but be careful," Fred said.

We approached the alley with great caution, but there was no need to. We saw them almost immediately. It was most of my hired muscle.

Four of my bullies all sat next to each other right in the middle of the alley and two others stood nearby. We jogged over to them and I swore under my breath when I was close enough to see them clearly. Little Paul, the

Hutt, Kevin, and iBully were all tied up on the ground. Some were crying. Only Snapper and PrepSchool were not bound, but they still looked pretty shaken. They were trying to untie the others, unsuccessfully. I knew immediately what had happened. I had ordered a hit on Staples's hit man, so he responded by ordering a hit on *my* hit men.

"Help us, Mac," Kevin said. Kevin was a seventh grader. A real tough kid, actually, and now his eyes were red from crying.

We freed the four of them and they all rubbed their wrists and tried to soothe their injured pride. These were the kings of the school and they had just been manhandled and made fools of. They weren't even angry; they all looked more scared than anything else.

I addressed the Hutt, as he seemed to be the only one who could talk without crying or stumbling over a busted lip.

"How did this happen?" I asked.

"They were jus' there waitin' for us," the Hutt said.

"Who?"

"It was a bunch a' high schoolers and Justin Johnston. I was on my way home when these two high school kids grabbed me and forced me here. And then when I got here, they tied me up and then they brought everybody else here, too. There were like four or five high school kids and Justin and his friend Mitch. They, like, punched us and kicked us and, uh, we tried to get free and fight back, but we couldn't. The only one of us who even got a hit on one of them was Snapper. She bit one of them in the ear because they refused to fight her, due to her being a girl and all." The Hutt practically choked on his panic. "They said to give you a message, too."

"What?"

"They said we're all outta commission. They also said that you were next. They said that you're a dead man for not giving up Fred and for what you did today."

I kept silent and tried to look calm. If I showed my fear, then we'd be doomed. People always turned to me last for help, and if I was too scared to help them, then . . . well . . .

"I told you Staples was bad," Fred said with wide eyes.

"I'm sorry, Mac, but I'm out. I quit. I don't care how much money you give me," the Hutt said.

The other bullies agreed.

We tried to convince them otherwise, but in the end all six of them quit right then and there. Which was probably for the better. I had gotten them hurt already. If they kept working for me, who knows what could happen to them. I needed to deal with this myself. I couldn't risk any more innocent kids getting hurt. Compared to

Staples, even the bullies were innocent.

We were careful the rest of the way home, but there was no sign of trouble. Someone was obviously toying with me, stabbing me in the back, selling me up the river, double-crossing me, two-timing me, or whatever else you want to call it. Someone was feeding Staples inside information. He just knew too much.

That night, after I convinced my dad that I was finished with my homework, I went over to Vince's house to discuss a plan to oust the rat. As much as going to Vince's at night creeped me out due to its proximity to the Creek, I still tried to go over there once in a while so he didn't feel bad about where he lived.

We sat in his bedroom and played video games while we talked. I loved his room because it was covered in Cubs stuff. Posters; a framed, autographed jersey that we had bought a few years ago with our profits; banners; baseball cards. He even had Cubs sheets on his bed. He had one amazing poster that was like this panoramic shot of Wrigley Field. You could never go wrong brainstorming under the gaze of so much Cubs stuff.

"Staples clearly has an informant, someone close to our operation," I said. "Given the exchange Joe and I saw between Brady and Jacky Boy earlier, I think it's pretty obvious who the number one suspect is. Brady likely owes Staples a bunch of money and is now spying on us to help repay it."

Vince nodded, but Joe seemed less certain.

"I'd be careful jumping to conclusions, Mac. It could just be a coincidence. We really shouldn't assume anything. We need to be sure before we do anything drastic," Joe said.

"Joe's right, Mac," Vince said. "How do we know Brady wasn't arguing on our behalf? Maybe they were arguing about Jacky Boy taking bets. Plus, we can't forget Nubby, Great White, and Kitten as suspects."

I nodded. They were both right, of course. I was just so ready to wrap up this problem and move on to the bigger issue of taking down Staples himself that I was rushing myself and jumping to conclusions. I'd forgotten about the fact that the other three bullies weren't ambushed. Was that just a coincidence? Or did it mean something more? Outside of Kitten, who I was pretty sure would never side with Staples, these weren't exactly the most trustworthy kids to have working for you.

"Yeah, those are good points. This whole thing is a much bigger mess than I thought," I said. "One thing is clear, though. We need to figure out who the mole is before we move ahead with any other plans. Because as long as Staples knows what we're up to, we've got no shot at winning."

With that the three of us came up with a way to verify just who the snitch might be. It wasn't something I wanted to do. In fact, what we'd be doing tomorrow would get us expelled immediately if we were caught. But it was a necessary risk; we needed to know who was leaking information, and we needed to know soon.

Chapter 12

The next morning Joe and Vince met me in my office before school like we'd planned the night before. We chose a time so early it was still dark outside. As much as our bloodshot eyes hated us for that, it was essential that we not be seen doing what we were about to do or we could all kiss our futures good-bye. Expulsion doesn't look good on permanent records, even if the importance of those things is a little overblown by adults.

We put on ski masks in case we *were* caught. Then we'd still have a chance to run and possibly get away without being identified. We nodded at one another and left my office, creeping through the halls, staying low and close to the walls.

Soon we arrived at the fourth-grade locker bay. I looked at a printout of locker assignments that I'd acquired earlier this year by helping out an administration office student assistant with a problem involving her parents and some boy who apparently had really dreamy eyes. We stopped in front of our target's locker.

"You have the key?" Joe asked me.

"No, we came all this way and I forgot to check," I said.

Joe rolled his eyes. "I was just asking."

I smiled at him and held up the small brass-colored key. Vince and Joe nodded, but if there is such a thing as a nervous nod, those were it. We all knew how serious searching through another kid's locker is. Especially if you broke in by using the master key. That's right. I was holding the master key to every locker in the school.

How did I get such a key? Well, there's actually a pretty cool story that explains it all, how I got my office and keys to the school and all sorts of other perks, such as the locker master key. Remember how I said before that I'm in tight with the janitor? Well, it's kind of a long story, but I don't think you'll mind.

It all started a couple years ago. At that time, I didn't have the cool office in the East Wing boys' bathroom. Back then we operated our business inside two giant tires on the far side of the grade school playground. It wasn't much. I mean, it was just two huge tires that they stuck in the ground for kids to climb on. But it did the job. The tires were pretty big and they provided just enough privacy for us to run our business. Of course, back then things were much simpler. We didn't handle the same sorts of problems, and the tires were really all we needed. To be honest, a lot was different back in those days. I even had a different strongman; we called him Bazan. The story of what happened to good old Bazan is pretty long and complicated itself, so I'll leave that for some other time.

Anyways, like I was saying, back then business was pretty simple. I worked out of the tires with Vince and Bazan and mostly just handled easy stuff like writing kids notes to give to their crushes or maybe getting them snacks that their parents wouldn't buy for them. Young kids had a lot of simple problems that they just couldn't solve themselves, so business was booming. But it was booming in a small sort of way because they also didn't have much money.

About that time, the school was experiencing some problems of its own. It seemed that some kid had been splattering the school with graffiti. It was everywhere: in the bathrooms, on the sides of the building, on lockers, on walls, on the trophy case. The artist even managed to tag the principal's door. The coolest part was that the graffiti wasn't lame stuff like a name or a dumb saying; it was actually really awesome caricatures of all the school's teachers and staff like the lunch ladies and counselor.

The drawings were really funny. They always pointed out the teacher's funniest parts. Like Mr. Dickerson. The graffiti version had a really huge balding head and big creepy eyes, just like the real Mr. Dickerson. One of the math teachers, Mr. Thompson, had two big front teeth, and his graffiti picture had even bigger front teeth and little bunny ears. My personal favorite was this drawing of a history teacher named Mr. Ritter. Mr. Ritter had thick, huge fingers, and in the graffiti drawing his fingers were giant sausages. Everybody started calling him Sausage Fingers. It was a little obvious but still pretty hilarious. Pretty much all the kids loved the graffiti drawings. But of course the teachers really hated them.

After a few weeks the artist had drawn almost all of the school's staff and still hadn't been caught. It's pretty amazing, really, especially with all the teachers on high alert. He was so good at not getting caught that all the kids started calling him the Graffiti Ninja. Not even the students knew his real identity.

After this had gone on for a while, the school began to put serious pressure on the janitor to clean up all of the graffiti as soon as possible. The problem was that the

Graffiti Ninja used a Magnum 44 marker to do his drawings. I don't know if you've ever seen a Magnum 44 marker, but they're huge. They're, like, almost the size of a baseball bat practically. And they smell like a billion chemicals all mixed together with gasoline. The ink is almost impossible to wash off. In fact, to this day, you can still see the faint outlines of some of the Graffiti Ninja's work.

So the janitor was getting pretty frustrated. It wasn't easy cleaning up graffiti all the time, not to mention all the usual stuff he had to clean around the school like toilets and whatnot. He didn't know where to turn. And I suppose that's why he eventually came to me. That's why most people came to me, because they didn't know what else to do.

I'm still not entirely sure how he found out who I was and what I did. I know he had a son who was just a few years older than me. So it's likely that one night when the janitor was crying during dinner or something because of all the stress he'd had lately because of the Graffiti Ninja, his son told him about Vince's and my business. That's how I always imagined it went, anyways.

Either way, the point is that the janitor did come to me for help. And I have to say he looked pretty funny, too, with his legs folded under him like a pretzel, crammed inside the giant tire like a foot-long hot dog in a regular-sized bun.

"So what can I do for you?" I asked him after Vince gave me a nod and walked back to his post outside the tire. I touched my fingertips together in front of me like I was holding a sub sandwich and was about to take a bite.

He looked like he was trying to hide a smirk. That was okay, though. Adults never take little kids seriously. I was used to it.

"Well, I want you to find the kid who has been making those drawings all over the school. And I'd *really* like it if you could somehow get him to stop," he said.

I nodded and tapped my fingers together.

"That would be quite a challenge," I said.

The janitor was smirking again. I ignored it.

"You *do* know that my services are not free, yes? Especially for a favor of this magnitude."

"Oh, oh yes. Yes, I'm well aware of that, thank you, Mac," he said, still smiling.

"Okay, then, I think I may be able to help, but I can't guarantee anything. I'll see what I can do and then I'll contact you later. How does that sound?"

"That sounds good. Thanks again, Mac," he said.

But he said it in that way that adults sometimes talk to kids. You know, how they draw out each word and then make it high pitched on the end. Like they're saying, "Oh, you're so cute because you're a kid and I know that whatever you say doesn't really matter." That's kind of how he spoke to me. But I didn't care. I knew the best way to get him to take me seriously was to just go and solve his problem.

So that's what I did.

The first step was to call a meeting. I had Bazan and Vince round up a huge group of kids to meet me by the large tires. There were probably about ten kids total and they were all gossip girls, kids on the junior debate team, ballet dancers, kids who loved James Bond movies, nosy kids—basically everybody who I thought would be good at either gathering information or sneaking up on people.

"Okay, I've gathered you all here because I have a mission for you. A mission for which you will be paid very well," I said. A murmur rippled through the kids. Grade school kids do not get money very often, unless they have an allowance or a paper route and those only get them so far. "The mission is for you to discover the identity of the Graffiti Ninja."

This time they erupted in conversation. It was like I had just told them to find out whether or not aliens really existed. It was a task thought to be impossible, and a little silly.

"How are we, like, supposed to do that, or whatever?" one of the gossip girls asked.

"*You* just need to do what you do best: Find the

gossip, find the dirt. You ballet dancers sneak around all day and try to catch him in the act. Debate kids, you grill everybody you come across. Nosy kids, you spy on everybody and anybody; look for inky fingers or Magnum-sized bulges in backpacks. And all of you just keep your eyes and ears peeled. If we all do this together, then we *will* find out who it is," I said.

They stood there looking at me.

"Okay, you can all go earn your money now," I said, and clapped a few times. The group slowly dissipated.

I turned to Vince after they were all gone.

"What do you think?"

"I think that I'd like some peanut butter ice cream right now," he said with a concerned look on his face.

I smiled. "I'm serious, Vince. Do you think they have a chance?"

"I'm serious, too, Mac. I love PB ice cream."

I laughed.

"Honestly, Mac, I'm not sure if they do have a chance. I think you should look into getting some extra help," he said.

Leave it to Vince to give it to me straight. I wasn't sure what else there was I could do, but Vince had a way of always being right that was both annoying on one level but also super beneficial to the success of our business.

"What did you have in mind?"

"I think you need to think outside the box, do something drastic. The normal tricks might not be enough for a problem this difficult."

I looked at him and raised my eyebrows. "You mean . . ." I started.

"Yup. I think you should go talk to Tyrell Alishouse. Because I think this is going to be a make-it-or-break-it thing for our business. We're paying these kids a lot of money, and this is a high-profile gig. No reason to hold back now." Vince turned and hopped inside the large tire to rework our Books. Just like that, Vince had casually suggested a course of action that would drastically change the face of our business for the better for years to come. That's why whenever we disagree on something, I usually end up coming around to his argument.

In the end, I wasn't sure just how "make-it-or-break-it" this case was, but it definitely was the most massive and expensive mission I had ever undertaken. And Vince almost never steers me wrong, so I took his advice and went to go see Tyrell.

Tyrell Alishouse is this kid obsessed with spying on people and lurking in the shadows and stuff like that. Most kids avoid him because they think he's a creepy weirdo, and he avoids most people because you can't be a spy if you're always being seen. His idols are Nancy

Drew, James Bond, some guy named Shaft, and two dudes called the Hardy Boys. I understand why a lot of kids avoid him—he *is* pretty strange. But Vince and I know better.

I spotted him in the bushes out near the faculty parking lot that afternoon recess.

"Hey, your name is Tyrell, right?" I said.

His head popped up from the bushes like a gopher, with one finger pressed against his lips. Then he motioned for me to join him. I climbed back to where he was, wedged between the bushes and the school building.

"I need your help," I whispered. I had no idea why I had to be quiet, but I didn't want to mess up whatever sort of sting he had going on.

"You're that problem solver guy, right? MacGyver?" he whispered back.

"Yeah."

He nodded. "I thought you might be looking for me."

"How did you know?" I asked.

"I heard you were starting a task force to track down the Graffiti Ninja," he said.

"But I only started it this morning; how could you know?" I asked.

"Because I was there," he said.

"But . . ."

He smiled. Then he shook his head. "The first thing

you need to know is I'm only seen when I want to be seen."

I knew right then that this kid and I were going to have a long and successful business relationship. I filled him in on what I needed and told him what the pay was for the job. He accepted without a moment's hesitation. I paid him more than anybody I had ever paid before, which I knew was risky, but without risk there's no reward. Or as Vince's grandma said once: Without Risk there's no such thing as Yakutsk.

And this time the risk paid off. Tyrell took to the challenge like my godfather, Bruce, to a bottle of moonshine. Slowly but surely the other kids on the task force began to bring me information. It was little things at first: The Graffiti Ninja was supposedly a sixth grader. She was a girl. She struck only during lunch and before school.

But it was Tyrell who busted the case wide open, just like I knew he would. I still don't know how Tyrell did it, but he somehow got an actual photograph of the Graffiti Ninja drawing a picture on the gymnasium floor. I remember how my jaw dropped when he showed me the photo inside my tire.

"How did you get this?" I asked.

"Sorry, Mac, but I can't reveal my methods," he said.

I looked at the photo again.

It turned out the Graffiti Ninja was this sixth grader

named Skylar Kuschel. People usually just called her Koosh because her name is funny and that's what kids do when people have odd names.

She's a pretty quiet kid, not too popular but not a complete dork either. She just kind of blended in with the crowd. I called a meeting with her and made a proposal: I would help her make money off her talents if she agreed to stop drawing on school property. I wouldn't even take a cut of the earnings. She agreed, and I set her up with a business selling personalized drawings to kids. Man, did she make a lot of money selling those things for a few years. She's in high school now, and I heard that she already has a few art schools that have been in touch with her. You'd think that the teachers might recognize her style, and maybe some even did, but in the end they had no proof that the Graffiti Ninja was her so there was nothing they could do anyway. Besides, teachers never suspect the "good kids" of troublemaking. Which is partially why Vince and I are able to get away with running our business right under everybody's noses.

Anyways, back to the janitor. After I made the deal with Koosh, I sent a message home with the janitor's son asking his dad to meet me. Still, I was kind of surprised when he showed up. I figured he thought I was too young to help him.

"Hey, thanks for coming," I said as he wedged himself inside the tire.

"Yeah, my son said that you had news for me," he said.

"I do, I do. I've found our graffiti artist," I said.

"Really?" the janitor asked. I could tell he was skeptical, but there was also a glimmer of hope in his eyes.

"And . . . I got her to stop drawing all over the school."

He was silent. He looked at me and shook his head. Then he let a huge smile spread across his face. Right then I could tell he's not like the other adults at the school.

"Are you serious?" he said.

I nodded. "Now it's all just a question of payment."

"Well, I have money, but . . . I think that I can offer you something a little more valuable."

"I'm listening," I said.

"Well, there's this bathroom in the East Wing. It's missing a toilet, has some plumbing problems, and is way back by the old band room, which is just a storage room now, so hardly anyone ever uses it. I still don't know why they even put a bathroom back there in the first place, but I stopped asking the administration those types of questions a long time ago. It's like asking a gerbil to explain quantum physics. Anyways, I was going to recommend to the school that this bathroom be closed down permanently . . . . But I think it might be of better use to you. Think of it as your new office. What do you say?" He smiled, a set of keys dangling from his hand.

"Are *you* serious?" I said. I didn't think adults could be this cool. Especially not ones who work for the school.

"I sure am, Mac. You're saving me a huge headache by getting that kid to stop drawing on the school. It's the least I can do."

"Deal." I took the keys and shook his hand.

The East Wing bathroom is a safe place to have an office because, really, the janitor is the only school official ever to go in that bathroom. Dickerson never would because of his unfortunate toilet seat incident, and all the other teachers have their own cleaner, bigger bathrooms in the teachers' lounge, so I'm free and clear. And the students don't complain either. Our business helps them out, and like I said before, squealing is not allowed here. The best part was that once word got out that I had orchestrated the unmasking of the Graffiti Ninja, our business doubled. So that's how the janitor and I started our business relationship. He still comes to me for help from time to time to get kids to stop putting gum under their chairs and stuff like that.

So I can get pretty much any key I want from the janitor, no problem, no questions.

But that's kind of what made this particular mission so dangerous. If we got caught in the school before it opened, I could potentially get the janitor fired and us expelled. Which would be about the last thing I'd ever want to see happen.

"Hurry up, Mac!" Vince whispered.

I nodded and slid the key into the small slot on the combination dial. I had to wiggle the key a little as I turned it, but eventually a metallic click was followed by the creak of the locker door swinging open. We were in.

I wasn't sure exactly what we'd find, but I remembered from my meeting with Jacky Boy that he carried around a notebook of all the bets he'd taken. I just hoped he kept it at school. His locker was a disaster, and we found a surprising amount of loose dollar bills and, oddly enough, a nice collection of little bundles of hair of all different colors. We looked at one another, resisted the urge to ask because none of us actually wanted to know, and then kept searching.

Then I found it. Nestled way in the back behind a huge geography textbook. His little notebook. We flipped it open and scanned the pages together using a small flashlight. When we got to page thirteen, that's when we saw it.

Brady's name. And next to it a staggering dollar amount with a negative symbol in front of it. Then right after that in parentheses Jacky Boy had scribbled, *Doesn't have the money, will pay back with major favor.*

We didn't want to believe it, but it doesn't get much clearer than that. Brady was our snitch. How could I have been so stupid? I blamed myself, really, for the information leak. The general rule was never to let anyone outside the business know what you're thinking. And I had broken that rule by bringing in Brady.

"The little snitch. We should do to him what Ronald McDonald does to ketchup packets," Vince said. From the look in his eyes I could tell it wasn't a joke. That's the thing about Vince that only I know: Most of the time when people think he's only joking around, he actually is being serious.

Joe laughed, but he didn't sound all that amused. "We should make copies of this book."

I was just about to agree when the hallway lights flicked on. We froze. That meant it was 7:05. Teachers would be showing up any minute. There just wasn't time. We shoved the book back into its hiding spot, slammed the locker shut, and took off sprinting toward the nearest exit. After removing our masks, we circled the block and came back in through another door as if we were just arriving.

Chapter 13

Later that day at lunch Joe escorted Brady into my office. I'd had to fire someone only once before and it hadn't been pleasant. Plus, I still liked Brady. I couldn't believe he would double-cross us like that.

"What's up, Mac? Why's everyone acting so serious?" he asked as he sat down.

"The jig is up, Brady. It's over," I said.

He shook his head and furrowed his brow.

"Don't play dumb, Brady. I know what you've been doing," I said.

"Mac, I . . . I'm not sure what you mean," he said slowly.

"I think you *do* know," I said. "And it's over. You're fired."

"Why are you doing this, Mac? What about Fred? Who will watch over him? I need to be here. I need this job, Mac!" he said. His face fell, and I could tell he was dropping the act. "I admit that I got into a bit of trouble. I mean, I guess I owe a lot of money to Staples. But I swear I'm on your side! That's *why* I'm on your side. I can't ever pay back what I owe, so my only chance is to help you take out Staples before he takes me out."

"You know what?" I asked him. "I just don't care. I'm sick of being lied to. Whether you're telling the truth or not, I just can't trust you anymore."

"But," he started, and then seemed to give up. He knew he was had.

"Good-bye," I said coldly.

I wanted him to break down. I didn't feel comfortable punishing him any further without a full confession. But he just started crying tears of guilt and buried his face in his hands. I nodded at Joe. He lifted Brady out of the chair and escorted him out of the bathroom.

I spent the rest of lunch convincing Great White, Nubby, and Kitten to stay on board with our business after what had happened to the other bullies. Then I told them all about the rat and note I found in my locker. I wanted everybody to be extra careful, just in case. To try and stick together as often as possible. And I agreed to up their pay a little in light of the increased danger of working for me.

At afternoon recess I organized another meeting between Joe, Vince, and me that night at Vince's place. It was probably an especially dangerous time for us to be meeting near the Creek, given the threats we'd received, but it was also important that we rotate our meeting places. Besides, it was kind of fun to visit my old trailer park once in a while. The purpose of this meeting was to move up the ladder. Now that we had our snitch situation taken care of, it was time to strike a real blow against Staples.

"We need a new plan," I said as the three of us played video games in Vince's room. "I think we need to go straight to the top this time."

"What! We can't go after Staples—we'd get wasted! I heard he's got a pit bull chained up near his office," Joe said.

"You're right. That'd be crazy; we don't even know how to get to Staples. We don't know what he looks like or where he lives. But we can go after Justin Johnston. He runs the business at our school and without him Staples will have nothing here. He takes the money and bets. I bet he also does some of the bribing of athletes and stuff, too. I think that if we take out Justin, we can deal Staples's business a pretty good blow," I said.

"Let's do it," Vince said.

"What are we going to do, though?" Joe asked as in the video game I got my revenge by dropping a grenade onto his character after he walked into my trap.

"I don't know. You guys got any ideas?" I said.

"Mac, that's perfect!" Vince yelled. "What you just did to Joe in the game, I mean. We should do the same thing to Justin Johnston. It'll be like when Ronald Reagan was so obsessed with "Star Wars" that he totally blew the U.S.'s chances of getting out of the Cold War before nineteen ninety."

I shook my head and sighed. Vince references history stuff a lot. He's really good at school and reads a lot of huge dusty books from the nonfiction section of the library that I wouldn't touch with a ten-foot pole.

Vince grinned at me and said, "Just try to imagine a chimpanzee named Bonzo with strings attached to his hands and feet like a puppet and it'll make sense."

I laughed, but of course it still didn't make any sense at all. Once Vince started pulling out monkey references, it was time to move on or he'd start saying some really bizarre stuff.

"Look, guys, I hate to interrupt, but even if we do trap Justin, what are we actually going to do to him? We can't exactly blow him up with a grenade like in the game," Joe said.

"We'll make him an offer he can't refuse," I said.

Like I said, I always try to say that as often as possible. I love that movie. I think it's called *The Godfather*, but it doesn't have any pizza in it and it isn't about some guy's crazy godparents or anything, so don't let the title mislead you. I know I'd never want to watch a movie about my godfather, Uncle Bruce. He smells funny, like a hospital specializing in chemical burns, and he always punches me on the arm and calls me kiddo like we're in some lame TV show on Disney. Once during a family reunion, I saw my uncle Bruce peeing off the balcony of his hotel room. I heard my parents say something about him falling off a wagon. I think maybe he hit his head pretty hard when he fell off that wagon and is now brain damaged or something.

"What does that mean, 'an offer he can't refuse'? You're always saying weird stuff like that," Joe said, but he was laughing. "I swear, sometimes I think you two are the strangest kids on earth."

I grinned. It was times like that that I realized how close Joe was to becoming an adult. Vince and I spent the next few minutes filling Joe in on what we had in mind. And I have to say that it was a pretty good plan. Vince and I smiled at each other as we discussed it, and even Joe was smiling by the time we'd finished explaining it.

But then I wasn't sure if Vince was smiling because

he liked the plan or because he had just snuck up behind me in the video game and swiftly stabbed my character in the back.

We hung out and played video games for another hour or so. Then Joe had to leave.

"What are you guys doing this weekend?" he asked as he put on his jacket.

"We're going to the lake with my family," I said. "So take the weekend off."

"All right, sounds good," he said.

Vince and I still had to find time to start planning the trip, with everything else going on, and this seemed like a good chance to start. Normally, talking about the Cubs winning a series before they actually do would be a huge jinx, and we probably *were* ruining it for all Cubs fans right then and there in Vince's room. But it was a necessity for us. Two sixth graders just can't up and go to a World Series game on the spur of the moment. An event as sacred as a Cubs World Series required careful planning. It went above the jinx.

"So you think that we should just go cheap and sit in the nosebleeds or try to go all out and sit in the lower section?" I asked.

"I want awesome tickets, of course, but we can't afford them with you handing out our money like political pamphlets. The good ones are going for over twenty-seven hundred bucks apiece right now! We may not even be able to get the cheap seats at this rate," Vince said. "That's so much money, Mac. I mean, just think about it."

"I know that's a lot, Vince, but what choice have I had? We're in this for the long haul now; I don't think we can back out. Besides, the bullies have helped us. We're close to ending this whole thing."

"Maybe," Vince said, but it didn't seem like he was really even thinking about the Cubs game anymore. He was just kind of looking out the window with eyes that resembled glazed donut holes. What was with him lately? I guess the stress of this Staples business was really getting to him.

"Which game should we try for? One? Seven?" I asked.

Vince pondered this with the same glassy-eyed stare he'd had for much of the night. Then he finally said, "I think we should just go for the first game, because what if the Cubs choke like they always do and get swept? Then there won't be a game seven and we'll miss our only chance to see a World Series game at Wrigley. Possibly forever."

I nodded.

I know it must seem like we were pretty negative fans, but that's the way you're supposed to think if you're a Cubs fan. Otherwise, you'd just get your heart broken again and again and again.

Right now you're probably thinking: No way. There's no way this little sixth grader could have enough money to buy two tickets to a game this expensive. And you know what? It *does* seem a little ridiculous. But Vince is a great business manager. He kept us on track saving money religiously for over four years. And the business did pretty well, so there was a lot of money to save. Besides, we also get money for allowance and birthdays, too. Plus, we have no bills to pay, like for cars or rent, nothing outside of our normal business expenses. Add all that up, and we'd amassed a pretty large pile of cash inside my closet.

How much?

Well, Vince would be the guy to tell you for sure, because he's the one who kept track, but I believe at that time the two Funds combined with our regular savings would have equaled about six thousand dollars. Which is totally, mind-bogglingly crazy, but we did run a pretty tight little operation, like I said before.

"Well, we should probably worry about getting rid of Staples before we worry about what seats to buy, because if we don't do that, then there won't be a Cubs game for us at all," I said.

"I think this new plan will work, though. It's kind of like my grandma says, 'There ain't no use whining like a sharecropper when it's raining raisins and acrobats.'"

"Gross," I said, but laughed anyway.

"Okay, Mac, I've got it," Vince said.

"What, you know a better way to take out Staples's operation?" I asked hopefully.

Vince smiled. "No, no. I've got a Cubs question that's sure to crown me champion. Ready?"

I nodded and rubbed my temple.

"On what day and against what pitcher did Ernie Banks get his five-hundredth home run?"

"Ooh, tricky . . . I know that it was May twelfth, nineteen seventy, against Atlanta, but the pitcher . . . That's not really a fair multiple-part question, Vince. It's like two separate questions!" I said.

"Hey, remember that time you hit me with a double question on Ron Santo?"

He had a good point. I resumed rubbing my temple and closed my eyes.

After a few moments I smiled. "Pat Jarvis."

Vince shook his head in defeat. "I really thought I had you that time."

"All right, I better go. It's getting late. I'll see you tomorrow. Remember, we're leaving around seven in the morning for the lake cabin," I said. My parents rented a lake cabin a few weekends every year and they usually let me bring Vince with.

"Okay, Mac, see you."

Outside I hopped on my bike. It was fall, so it was already dark even though it was only eight o'clock. That made it especially creepy being this close to the Creek. I cut through an alley across from Vince's trailer park because it was a shorter route to my house. That's when two headlights popped up behind me.

I turned and looked back; some car was turning into the alley. Perfect timing, I thought as my eyes squinted into the bright lights. I turned into someone's back driveway to let the car pass through because there wasn't room for a bike and a car in the narrow alley.

But it didn't go. It just sat there at the entrance with its lights on and its engine running. I wondered if it was waiting for me to go through first. I decided that must be the case and rode back into the alley. Then I heard gravel crunch behind me as the car started driving forward.

What was this jerk doing?

The car's headlights flicked a much brighter shade of whitish blue and blinded me. I heard the engine rev and the car surged forward even faster. I remembered the note from the locker saying I'd be roadkill if I didn't hand over Fred. My heart began beating so fast and so high in my chest that it felt like I was choking on it.

I turned and pedaled, pushing as hard as I could as the car gained on me. There were six-foot wooden fences on either side of me. Nowhere to go but the end of the alley or the underside of the car. My lungs pumped and my calves burned.

I heard the car just a few feet back now. I was a dead man, I knew it, but I put on a burst of speed and cleared the alley, turning right as sharply as I could onto the sidewalk. My bike slid underneath me and I fell on top of it onto the grass.

The car exited the alley and screeched to a halt as it tried to turn right with me. It was going too fast and fishtailed out into the middle of the street. Under the streetlights I could see that it was an older red sports car with faded black racing stripes on the hood. The windows were tinted and I couldn't see who was driving it. But I didn't really have time to examine any closer, because the car suddenly lurched forward and then turned to face me.

I quickly got back on my bike and drove toward my house as the car bounced up onto the sidewalk after me. I couldn't believe it; the driver was actually trying to hit me. I felt the headlights engulf me as the car got closer. He was driving up on the sidewalk and even on people's yards. I envisioned myself being crushed underneath an old sports car on somebody's front lawn while the family inside grouped around the window and watched. They would all be drinking huge cups of hot cocoa.

I shook off the image and veered my bike across somebody's front yard and around to the back of the house where there wasn't room for the car to follow. I tried to stay low as I rode through that alley and then through another yard. Zigzagging madly through alleys and yards, I made my way toward my house. The car drove by a few times, but each time I was able to duck behind a fence or trash can. It also helped that there were no streetlights in the alleys.

Eventually I drove up the sidewalk to my house. I typed in the code for our garage and it opened, spilling light onto the driveway. As I walked my bike inside, I heard a car screech to a halt right in front of my house. The red sports car sat there under the streetlamp with its headlights still on. I could feel the driver staring at me. I looked right to where I thought his head would be and stared back. It was pretty safe inside my garage but a chill went up my spine anyways. The car sat there for at least two minutes. Then my dad came into the garage and the red car drove away.

"Hey, who was that?" he asked.

"I don't know. I think it was some pizza guy looking for a house," I said.

He nodded. "Close the garage door. You're letting bugs in." He went back inside.

I wanted to tell my dad. I really did. I mean, I always

try to keep my business and family separate but someone had just tried to kill me. There's nothing I wanted to
do more right then than to tell my parents.

But I still couldn't say anything. The Cubs game is
too important and getting my parents involved would
only risk us not being able to go. For one, they'd call
the cops and once the cops got involved I'd run the risk
of having to come clean about my Funds. No adult was
going to let a kid keep six grand in his closet. Also, if
my parents thought that someone was out to kill me,
then they'd go into super overprotective mode. Which
means they'd definitely nix our plan to go to Chicago
with Vince's brother.

I wanted my parents' help, but this was something
I would have to deal with myself. It was the only way.
Besides, this wasn't my parents' problem. It was mine.
They had enough to worry about.

Chapter 14

On the car ride down to the lake cabin, I went through our Books and tried to figure out if I had any people who owed me a favor that I could use to help take down Staples. Vince sat beside me and read some ancient, dusty book about President Lincoln's Cabinet or something incredibly boring like that. He gets these books for like fifty cents each at the Salvation Army store. I can never understand how he reads that stuff without falling asleep.

I hadn't slept well the night before so it was hard to stay awake on the drive there. I'd kept thinking I heard a car drive slowly past the front of my house. It was probably a different car each time, but I still couldn't get the image out of my head of the sinister red sports car creeping past again and again, its tinted windows revealing nothing but the reflections of tall evergreens.

"So you really think the plan to take out Justin will work?" I asked Vince as we later cast our lines out into the water. It was Saturday morning after we'd arrived, and we were sitting side-by-side on the end of the dock.

"I don't know. It has to; he'll have no choice. I just don't know if taking out Justin will get rid of Staples, you know? The U.S. put Castro into office in Cuba to get rid of the old dictator, but then they ended up having even bigger problems with Castro. You just can't be sure."

"Huh?" I said.

Vince laughed. "What I mean is we might solve one problem but that just may create another. Like, what if taking out Justin only motivates Staples more than ever to take us out?"

"Maybe we should just call the cops," I suggested.

"We could, but what would we say? 'Hey, this is some kid and I want to report this guy for running a gambling ring inside my school. And he also attacks us with his car and leaves rodents in our lockers. Oh yeah. I also don't know his real name or what he looks like. I don't even know his age. But please, officer, get right on that!'"

"Good point," I said.

We sat in silence for a few minutes.

"Want to know what my grandma might say at a time like this?" Vince asked.

I grinned. "Of course."

"She'd say, 'Sometimes I wish I was a manatee.'"

I laughed. She probably would say that, too. Seriously, Vince's grandma is such a riot, despite also being really cranky.

After lunch that day we played catch. Vince brought up our financials right away. I think he thought I was blowing our chances of getting to the Cubs game by paying everybody so much to help us. I wanted to agree with him, but I hadn't really had much of a choice.

"Let's be honest, Mac. From the beginning you've been more worried about outdoing Staples than simply protecting Fred. This isn't a contest about whose business is better or anything like that. Sometimes I think you forget why we started this business and our Funds in the first place," he said.

"I've only done what I've had to," I said. "It's called confronting a problem."

Vince gave me one of his looks and then threw me a fastball. Thankfully, I caught it in the webbing of my glove and not on the palm. He'd put some real heat on that one. I was a little annoyed about his implied accusation that I was more concerned about beating Staples than going to the game.

I threw a lazy curveball. He caught it without saying anything and threw me a circle change that I almost dropped. Silence isn't like Vince when he's around me. I could tell he was upset, and it was really irritating me. I know this will sound totally cheesy, but I kind of missed him even though we were together all the time. He was right here with me, but he might as well have been hanging out at the Great Wall of China.

"I think I may have you," I finally said, getting tired of doing all the talking.

Vince raised his eyebrows. "We'll see."

"What was the original name of Wrigley Field?"

"Weegham Park. Easy," Vince said as he caught my floating slider that broke all of half an inch.

I shrugged. It was going to be impossible to stump this kid. That's probably why I hadn't been able to do it in the two years we'd been doing trivia. Not like it mattered at that point. Honestly, I was too busy obsessing over why Vince had been acting so distant lately to come up with a better question. There had to be more to this than simply my spending too much money. I mean, for him to answer a Cubs question right and not do any gloating afterward is like a girl in my class leaving a shopping mall empty-handed.

We threw the ball back and forth in silence for a while. The air felt heavy, like we were in a giant sauna. I knew we were both thinking the same thing: What went wrong? It seemed like this Staples thing had taken over every part of our lives. We couldn't even fully enjoy a simple trip to the lake anymore.

Plus, we had like only seven or eight days before we needed to buy tickets to the Cubs game, assuming they kept winning, and the tickets weren't going to buy themselves. I felt myself wishing that I'd just told Fred good luck and sent him on his way. Maybe Vince was right. Why did I always have to get involved? But what am I supposed to do? Ignore everyone who comes to me with an inconvenient problem? Where am I supposed to draw the line?

"How much money do we have right now anyways?" I asked Vince after a long silence that had been broken only by the muffled thumps of a baseball hitting leather.

"Why?" Vince asked. It was the fastest he'd responded to a question all weekend.

I held the ball for a bit and just looked at him. He looked worried, but then he smiled a smile so phony I could have seen it was fake if I was blindfolded.

"I'm just checking, that's all," I said.

"Oh. Well, I think we have just over six thousand or so," he said. Then he shook his head and rubbed his eyes. "No, wait. No, I guess it's more like just under six thousand. I think it's like roughly fifty-nine sixty-two all combined.

That's every dollar to our name. Or as my grandma would say, 'There ain't no place like Chattahoochee for making a lady feel like a carpetbagger.'" He laughed after saying this, but again it didn't sound quite like the Vince laugh I'd been used to hearing for the past seven years.

"Come on, Vince. That grandma quote isn't even close to making sense," I said while throwing him the ball. Normally, I would have laughed anyways, but I didn't feel much like laughing.

Vince caught the ball and shrugged without even cracking a smile and threw the ball back. Another nasty circle change that dropped off the table and this time I missed it. The ball bounced off the edge of my glove and hit my foot. It rolled under some trees a few feet away.

"Sorry, Mac," he said as I turned to get it.

"No problem," I said. "It was a good pitch."

Vince is going to be an awesome pitcher next summer when we finally get to play full-fledged fast-pitch baseball. Vince had been studying some Nolan Ryan book on pitching that he'd found at the Salvation Army, and ever since, whenever we play catch, we just throw different pitches at each other. I'm not nearly as good as Vince. Which is funny because in movies the guy who's good with math and reads a lot usually isn't all that good at sports. But Vince is good at everything. Except confrontations.

I leaned under a tree to get the ball and something caught my eye. It was an older red sports car. With faded black racing stripes. It was down the street and parked just off to the side of the road. I grabbed the baseball and stood up.

"What's wrong?" Vince asked, jogging over.

I motioned for him to follow me. We crept up to the next cabin over and peeked around the corner. It was definitely a red sports car, and it looked like the same one that had tried to run me down the night before. We could see it parked about a hundred yards down the gravel road in front of a small and dirty trailer that some mean lady lived in year-round. One time I drove a Jet Ski we'd rented too close to her dock and she came running out of her house screaming at me to get off her property, and then she threw a beer bottle at me.

"Is that the same car?" Vince whispered as we crouched behind the edge of the cabin.

"I think so. I can't believe he followed us here," I said.

"What should we do, Mac?" he asked.

"Doesn't your grandma have some advice for a situation like this?" I asked.

He rolled his eyes but actually grinned, which was nice to see.

"Let's get a closer look," I suggested.

Vince pondered this. I could tell he didn't want

to, but he finally nodded.

"You go first," he whispered.

I quickly ran from the edge of the cabin to a small tree across the gravel driveway. Vince followed. We moved closer to the car, hiding behind various objects: trash cans, trees, boats on trailers, central air-conditioning units. Finally I stopped behind a pine tree right next to the dirty trailer, about forty feet away from the car. I really thought it was the same one from the other night, but it was hard to tell because I had last seen it under the creepy, hazy orange glow of streetlights.

"You don't think that this place is Staples's headquarters, do you?" Vince asked.

"I don't think so; it's too far away from our school. Plus, I know the lady who lives here, and I think she lives alone."

We waited and watched. The car was empty.

"Well? Let's go!" Vince said, and started to run toward the car. But just then the trailer's front door slammed open with a bang that sounded like a gunshot.

Vince dove back behind the tree as if it actually was a gunshot. We ducked as low as we could. The tree was behind the front door a little bit, but it was only fifteen feet away.

A fat, balding guy came thundering out of the trailer. He wore an old, faded black shirt. His jeans were stained and holey. He looked to be about forty or so. He walked down the steps and across the lawn. Then we heard a woman screaming and he stopped.

"Don't come back, you drunken, lazy slob!"

"Yeah, don't worry about that!" he said, and headed for the car.

She came to the doorway of the trailer. "You're pathetic! Pathetic! Your son pays your bills, you useless piece of garbage! How embarrassing is that? No wonder your wife disappeared on you!" She slammed the door.

Vince and I both flinched.

The man just waved and kept walking toward the red sports car across the street. He got into the car and peeled away, spraying gravel and dust all over the lady's lawn. Once he was out of sight, we ran back to my cabin's backyard. After we caught our breath, we looked at each other.

"Guess it wasn't the same car," I said with a shrug.

"Nope," Vince said. "*Unless*, unless that old fat dude *is* Staples. I mean, the legends of Staples have been around forever, so maybe he really is that old now?"

I didn't think he was being serious. But it was possible. Maybe. Wouldn't Fred have said something, though? I realized that he'd never told me just how old Staples was.

Vince saw me thinking it over and then he rolled his eyes.

"Hey, Mac, I was kidding. You don't really think that was him, do you?" he said.

"I don't know. I mean, it does seem a little suspicious, right?"

"I guess, Mac, but this isn't a Charles Dickens novel," Vince said.

"What?"

"I mean, this is real life. Sometimes weird things happen. Events don't always have to connect perfectly or make sense. Like, the dude who was the fisherman at the beginning of the story doesn't always need to come back and also show up as the cobbler in the middle and then eventually be revealed to be the main character's long-lost uncle's cousin's former best friend's roommate who just so happens to be currently married to the main character's brother's friend's mailman. You know?"

"Maybe," I said.

"What other explanation is there? I think we both know that guy couldn't have been Staples. He was, like, forty. There's no way," Vince said.

"Yeah, that makes sense, but I'm almost sure that was the same car. What if . . . what if that was Staples's dad?" I said.

Vince looked at me for a moment, like he was thinking hard about what I said. "Mac, that really could be it. So that would mean Staples is doing all of this to help pay some of his dad's bills like that lady said."

"Yeah, I guess."

"That would change everything, don't you think?"

"Um, not really. Vince, I don't really care why he needs the money—that doesn't make it okay to cheat and swindle to get it."

"Well, maybe that kind of a situation would make a kid do crazy stuff he normally wouldn't do, right? I mean, how would *you* know what it's like for him?" Vince said.

"What's that supposed to mean?"

Vince just shrugged and gave me a look of his that said I should know what he meant.

"What's your problem lately, Vince? Look, I used to live in a trailer, too, remember? I know what it's like to not have a lot of money."

"Yeah, but do you still? Do you know what it's like for your family to *never* have a lot of money?"

"Whatever, Vince."

"Yeah, whatever is right," Vince said.

And that was that.

We got back from the lake cabin on Sunday evening around six. After dropping Vince off, we drove home. Vince and I hadn't talked a whole lot since that argument, and when we did, it was businesslike, as if we were doing it only because we had to. Really, I just didn't get what was up with him lately. It was like he was blaming me that his family still doesn't have a lot of money. As if I had anything to do with that. It's not like my family is rich or anything. Sure we have a house now and go on more vacations than we used to, but we aren't, like, driving around in luxury Italian sedans and telling the time with diamond-encrusted Rolex watches. I do feel a little bad that his family doesn't have as much, but Vince himself has plenty. Our business buys him basically whatever he wants.

As we drove up to our house, I heard my mom gasp. Then she swore, which she almost never does. My dad swore, too, but that isn't too unusual.

I looked up to see what all the commotion was.

It was our house. There were eggs all over it. I knew right away who had done it. I didn't even need to read the message they had crudely left in huge, red, spray-painted letters on the garage: "BacK oFF MaC or Your DeaD."

Poor spelling aside, it was pretty menacing. Mostly because I couldn't back off. If I gave up and just rolled over, then it would be easy for him to wipe us all out. So it wasn't really a threat. It was just meant to say: "You're dead, Mac." Which wasn't any better.

Chapter 15

The next morning as I left for school, I saw my dad on a ladder trying to scrub off congealing eggs. My mom pulled the car out of the garage and waited for me. I'd had her drive me to school ever since the night the red car tried to kill me. I couldn't risk riding my bike or walking to school anymore.

"Christian, are you sure that you have no idea who might have done this?" my dad asked, looking down at me. "You have no clue who this Mac character is?"

I felt like melting into the cracks on our sidewalk. My dad had so much work ahead of him and it was all my fault. But I still couldn't tell them, no matter how bad I felt. I had made a vow to keep my family and business separate and I meant to keep it.

"No, Dad," I said.

"Okay." He sighed.

I don't know if he believed me.

"I can help you with that after school," I said.

He thought it over. "Do you think you and some of your friends might want to come over and help clean it either today or tomorrow? I'll pay them and then maybe afterward they can come inside and watch a movie and have snacks."

"Sure, I'll ask them. They do love Mom's cookies," I said. Plus, we could always use more money; even if it was just like five or ten bucks. Five bucks would buy almost half a Chicago Dog at Wrigley Field.

"Okay, good," my dad said, and scanned the whole house from the ladder. "This is going to take a long time if I have to do it myself."

With that, he went back to scrubbing. My mom honked.

I slowly turned and walked to the car.

All morning customers were demanding cheaper prices because I had been so unavailable lately. And a few more came to me for loans to pay back gambling debts. Which was a problem because my funds were getting low. According to Vince, we don't have enough money to give out any more loans. The whole ordeal was embarrassing; I never turn away customers—it's against my business policy.

The worst part was that my cash flow was drying up because more and more of the customers who I actually could help had to pay with favors. It wouldn't be long before we would have to drain the Emergency Fund, and then eventually the Game Fund as well.

At the end of recess I instructed Joe to deliver a message to Justin during a class they had together right before lunch. The message was a proposal for a meeting to discuss business. I thought it sounded pretty political. At the end of the note I said Justin could choose the time and place, but it had to be on school grounds and it had to be this week.

Joe returned with only five minutes left in the lunch period. He handed me the note I'd given him earlier. I unfolded the crumpled piece of paper and looked at the bottom. Something had been written in blue ink. It was just four words: *Tomorrow, four, the Shed.*

The Shed is this little shack next to the school's track and football field. It's where the janitor keeps all of the yard work stuff like the lawn mower and sprinklers and other junk like that. It's also where all the kids who smoke gather during recess. The Shed is down the hill, across the football and baseball fields, and way out near the street, the chunk of school property farthest from the actual school building. It is a perfect place for kids to smoke because the recess supervisor on that side of the school hates walking, so she never really goes much past the first goalpost of the football field. They never get caught, and no one ever squeals on them, because squealing at our school gets you beat up. It's a pretty universal rule and we all follow it whether we want to or not.

I was already forming the second part of the plan. The Shed was actually a great place to have the meeting, because I could really use it to my advantage. All I needed was to get inside. It's kept locked at all times, but like I said before, I'm in tight with the janitor, so I knew he'd lend me the key for a few days. The plan was coming together rather nicely. Almost too well. In my experience, things just don't come this easily.

After reading Justin's response to my note, I looked up at Joe. He looked back, waiting for my reaction.

"It's on," I said.

He smiled.

"Go find the bullies and tell them to meet me in my office during afternoon recess," I said.

All I had to do now was brief the bullies and pay a visit to the janitor and our plan would be underway. Tomorrow. Four. The Shed. We'd be ready. And Justin Johnston would never see it coming.

Chapter 16

I knew that something was wrong the moment I got home from school that day.

As soon as I stepped through the door, my mom called out to me, "Christian, honey, you have a friend here in the kitchen."

I was immediately suspicious. All of my friends were at home; I had just parted ways with them a few minutes ago. Whoever was waiting for me in the kitchen, I had a feeling that it was not going to be someone I wanted to see.

I walked down the hallway, turned the corner, and there he was. I didn't know who he was at first, despite the fact that he looked kind of familiar. Or maybe deep down I really did know but just didn't want to believe it.

He sat at the kitchen table, looking like some kind of salesman. He wore a clean sweater and dress pants. But it was a bad disguise; you can't hide Staples's kind of menace from someone who knows what to look for. It would be like trying to disguise a lion by dressing it in a pink tutu. It's still going to eat you no matter what it's wearing.

Apparently, though, his clothes and smile had been enough to fool my mom into letting him into our kitchen. It probably didn't help that my mom is the kind of person who calls everyone sweetie or dear. She thinks everyone who uses polite words and a smile is a "nice young man." If my mom wasn't such a great cook, I'd say she's nuts.

Other than his neat and clean appearance, Staples was a monster. He was huger than huge, like the human version of a grizzly bear crossed with that shark from *Jaws* and a giant troll. And despite his dress clothes and smiling face, he still looked mean enough to eat little kittens and puppies like they were fruit snacks. His eyes bragged of inhuman intelligence. They were sharp, as if just a glance could gash your cheek like a razor blade. He was definitely still a teenager, but in the right lighting he could have easily passed for twenty-two. He had a shaved head with dark stubble for hair just starting to grow back. He also had the beginnings of a beard, every bit as prickly, dark, and menacing as his hair. His eyebrows were bushy and his jaw was square like a pro athlete on steroids. He smelled like cheap cologne. And if death and destruction had an odor, he would have smelled like that, too.

Something told me the smile on Staples's face was not there to make me feel better. And it didn't. A plate of Oreo cookies sat in front of him and he slowly brought one to his mouth and took a bite. I swear I heard the Oreo scream faintly as his teeth sank in.

I was still trying to convince myself that this was really happening, that Staples was really sitting at my kitchen table, when my mom came over and poured him a glass of milk. She smiled at me and winked. She clearly didn't know who she was dealing with. How could she? Staples probably *did* look like a nice guy to someone as trusting as my mom, someone who'd never heard any of the stories.

"Thank you, Mrs. Barrett," Staples said in a deep but polite voice.

My mouth opened, but no words came out. I tried to close it, but nothing happened. I thought my jaw was broken. I began to wonder if I'd ever be able to talk again. I panicked.

"Do you want some milk, Christian?" my mom asked.

"No . . . no thanks," I said, relieved that my jaw and

voice were working again.

"Okay, I'll give you and your friend some privacy, then." She left the kitchen.

I wanted to yell out for her to stay, but I didn't. This was between Staples and me, not my mom. I couldn't drag her into this.

"So we finally meet. I've been looking forward to this, Christian." Staples smiled. It was the sort of smile that a hyena might give a rotting zebra carcass.

He had also used my real name. Nobody but my family did that.

"Please, have a seat," he said, motioning to a chair across from him.

I sat down and tried to look calm. I was everything but calm. I was even afraid for my mom right now. I didn't think she could defend herself from this monster sitting in our kitchen.

Staples's smile grew wider. "It's really hot in here," he said, pulling at his sweater. "Do you mind?"

Without waiting for a response, he took off the sweater. He wore a simple white T-shirt underneath that revealed a pair of thick arms covered in tattoos. His arms were so muscular that his veins looked as if they were trying to escape his body. They wriggled like worms in rain with every movement of his hand. His tattoos covered his arms like second sleeves. One of them read "The Creek" in Old English–style lettering. But the others were all so bunched together that I couldn't even make them out.

"Do you know who I am?" he asked, and then took a drink of milk. It would have been much more fitting had it been a glass of blood.

I nodded but said nothing.

"What's the matter, cat got your tongue?" He had a small milk mustache.

I just looked at him.

He laughed. It was evil. But it also sounded easy, as if he laughed a lot.

"So you're going to sit there and act all tough, right? That's not a bad strategy. It might even work on some of the little wusses at your school. But I can see right through it, Christian." He gave me a stare that almost melted my bones. I half expected to turn into jelly and slide right off the chair onto the floor, forming a small pile of cowardly goo. But I just shrugged. That only made him laugh more. I thought I saw an Oreo cookie flinch as he reached out to grab another one off of the plate.

"Did your parents enjoy the decorating that we did this weekend?" he asked. It seemed as if he was having the time of his life.

"Yeah, the red paint went well with our white house.

Thanks," I managed to say as casually as I could.

He just laughed again.

"Did you like what we did to your Collector last week?" I asked, interrupting his laughter. I'd heard enough of it already.

He looked at me and his eyes turned black.

"You are a dead man, Christian," he said.

"Yeah, you've said that a few times now. Why am I still here, then? I know it was you who tried to run me over, and I still outran you. On my bike, no less," I said. I wished I would stop talking. I was only digging my grave even deeper.

Staples slammed his fist onto the table. The milk glass rattled and spun and almost tipped over before settling. An Oreo cookie flopped off the plate. We both looked at it and then he snatched it up and ate it in one bite.

After swallowing, he scoffed.

"Christian, Christian. I always did like to play with my food before eating it. I want to watch as your business crumbles right out from under you. I'll be there laughing as you cry because you've lost everything. Mark my words; you'll be left with no money, no employees, no business, and no friends. Then you'll realize how much you had and how much you've lost. And then, only then, after I've enjoyed your suffering for a while, will I finally destroy you," he said, leaning forward.

His eyes seemed to vibrate. His mouth twitched into a smile. Then he rubbed the corner of his left eye and sat back in his chair again.

"You really think you'll be able to do all that?" I asked, letting a grin sneak up to my lips.

Staples grinned back. His confidence was making me nervous. And you know how I feel about being nervous. What did he know that I didn't? What tricks were up his sleeve?

"I guess you'll just have to wait and find out," he finally said.

"Will I? Maybe just the opposite is happening. Maybe I'm taking *you* down, Staples."

He smirked.

"Oh, Christian. You've got guts—I'll give you that. You know, I could use a guy with your combination of brains and guts. I suppose I could hold off on destroying your life if you'd like to come and work for me instead? I think we could really help a lot of kids and make a lot of money if we joined forces, don't you think? Plus, that way, you'd get to live." He gave me a big smile.

I wondered if his offer was a trick or if he really wanted to work with me. Either way I'd refuse. I didn't like the sort of business he ran. Plus, he seemed a little too psychotic to be a good boss.

"No thanks," I said as calmly as I could.

"It's too bad you have to be so stubborn," he said. "I guess we're back to me destroying you, then. You're going to have paid dearly by the time I'm finished, too. You'll be wishing that you had never been born. That's a promise. And I don't break promises."

A long silence followed. It seemed like he was waiting for me to crack. Every once in a while he would snatch another cookie off of the plate and put it in his mouth. He always chewed slowly and quietly with his mouth closed. And his almost black eyes never left my face. Didn't this guy ever blink? After almost a few minutes he spoke again.

"It's too bad it had to be like this, Christian. You seem pretty smart. You remind me a lot of myself when I was in grade school."

"That's too bad," I said.

He laughed. He laughed for almost a minute while I just sat there.

"See? You're a funny guy, Christian. It's hard *not* to like you." As he said it, his fist closed around an Oreo he had been holding. It pulverized into a clumpy mess of cream filling and black crumbs.

I wanted him to stop using my real name. I kept looking at his facial hair. He had a beard and tattoos. How did I get involved in a war against this guy? How did I stand a chance?

"Well, I best be off now," Staples said. "My dog needs to be fed. Hey, did you know that pit bulls eat just about anything you feed them? Cool, huh?"

With that, Staples got up, finished his milk, and walked past me into the living room. I heard the front door open and close a few seconds later. He left me there with a half-empty plate of Oreos and a bunch of questions rattling around in my head like popcorn. Did he know about our plan? It seemed unlikely, but then again the timing of his visit was pretty suspicious. I really hated the thought that he might know more than I did. I had a bad feeling about the whole thing. But I'd find out tomorrow. If my plan worked, it would deal him a blow that he wasn't expecting.

My mom came back into the kitchen.

"Oh, your friend left. He seemed like such a nice young man," she said.

I rolled my eyes and reached for the plate of Oreos. If only she knew.

I spent that evening balancing out my Books for the new business we'd taken in that day. That was normally Vince's job, but I hadn't talked to Vince much that day. I guessed we were still a little mad at each other, though I still had no idea why he would be mad at me. I also hadn't really been able to stop thinking about Vince's answer to my question about our Funds at the lake cabin.

Plus, I was really starting to panic about the Cubs game. It would make me feel better to do a Funds check. To actually hold and see and count that kind of cash makes it feel more real. Usually whenever I'm worried about money for some reason or another, simply doing a Funds check makes me feel better, reminding me that it's still there, that all we worked for still exists and that a trip to a Cubs World Series game is actually possible.

Once my parents were asleep, I retrieved all of our Funds from the hiding spot in my room and began counting and verifying against the amounts I had in my Books.

It was near the end of counting that I realized something was off. A few days before at the lake Vince had said we had $5,962 all totaled. And that's what my Books worked out to as well. But once I added the Game and Emergency Funds along with what my books said we had in Tom Petty cash back at my office, we were short a few hundred bucks and change.

The Game Fund and Emergency Fund matched my Books. So that meant that the discrepancy was somewhere in the Tom Petty cash. The Tom Petty cash was basically all of our daily operations money. We heard some businessmen in this movie call some extra money "petty cash" once, so we decided to steal that name.

Tom Petty is actually some musician my dad listens to sometimes, and we decided just plain "petty cash" is too boring. It's like Vince sometimes says, "Why call a spade a spade when you can call it whatever you want?" Our Tom Petty cash was any money we used to make loans to kids, spend on business-related materials, pay employee salaries, etc. It's all the money we have and use that doesn't go into the Game or Emergency Funds.

This had to be an error with my Books. We'd been paying out so much lately, and with all this Staples commotion it'd be pretty easy to miss something, right? To forget to write something down? It had to be, because otherwise it meant someone was stealing cash from us. It certainly could have been Brady, given how many times we had left him alone in the office to watch Fred. But then again, the cashbox is hidden in the bathroom trash can and the only other two people who know where it is are Vince and Joe. And Vince and I are the only ones with a key to the box itself.

This is the reason I usually left the Books to Vince, to avoid headaches like this. I was going to have to figure this out tomorrow. Hopefully this was just a case of some bad bookkeeping on my part. But my brain kept wandering back to Vince's weird response to my question at the cabin. I chose to keep ignoring it.

Chapter 17

I called Vince before school that morning and told him to meet me at the office as soon as he could. I had no problem getting up early since I could barely sleep at all that night. Turns out, it's not as easy as it sounds just to assume something is a simple mistake and not a major problem.

I counted the Tom Petty cash before he got there and confirmed that we were short some money. When Vince finally arrived, I explained what I'd discovered the night before. He listened calmly the entire time and kept his eyes on the tile floor. When I finished, he nodded.

"So the two Funds worked out, though, right?" he asked.

"Yeah."

"Well, then I think everything is okay. I mean, we've been dishing out money left and right. My Books work out okay with your count from last night and this morning, so I bet you just forgot to write something down or messed up on the numbers somewhere in your Books."

I nodded. I was relieved to hear him say that but also surprised he wrote it off as a mistake so easily. How can he be so sure it wasn't his Books that were wrong?

"I guess," I said. "But can't we double-check your Books against mine, just to be sure? To see exactly where the mistake is? I'll feel better."

I started moving toward where he kept his Books in the first stall.

"Wait, Mac," he said quickly, and I stopped. "I mean, yeah, sure we can do that, but we have a bigger problem right now." Vince had a worried look on his face. "I can't make it."

"What?" I asked, not sure exactly what he meant.

"I can't make it to the meeting at the Shed after school today."

"Why not, Vince?" I asked. "Does this have something to do with what happened at the lake? Look, I'm sorry if I made you mad somehow. I don't know what I did, but whatever it was, I didn't mean to."

"No, it's not that," Vince said. "It's my grandma's, like, hundred-and-fiftieth birthday, or whatever, and I have to go to her apartment after school to 'celebrate.' I tried my best to get out of it, but my Mom . . ."

Vince's mom was a cool lady most of the time, but when she was set on something, it was impossible to get her to break. Impossible. Especially when it came to family stuff. She was obsessed with family.

"Wouldn't you have known about this sooner than now? I mean, her birthday is the same day every year, right?"

"Yeah, I just forgot. I don't have a good enough excuse to miss for my mom not to get suspicious, you know?"

"Well, I guess there's nothing you can do, then." Something didn't seem right about this.

"I'm so sorry, Mac. I begged, I pleaded . . . but my mom said stuff like, 'This'll probably be the last birthday you will ever get to celebrate with her!' Believe me, I'd much rather be there to see the look on Justin's face than to be at my grandma's place, which smells like cat pee, while she hits me over the head with her cane and tells me to 'sit up and speak louder' and says a bunch of crazy things that don't make sense."

I could tell that he felt pretty bad. But I also knew that he secretly *wanted* to go to his grandma's. He likes going over there.

"I already said it was fine. You don't really need to be there anyway," I said.

I looked at Vince and he glanced at my shoes. Was that guilt for having to bail or something else? I used to be able to read his face as easy as a picture book, but lately, it had been more like trying to read an organic chemistry book written in Russian.

Then the morning bell rang and ended our conversation.

It was in the middle of class that I realized my guts suddenly felt like quicksand, and I was melting into myself until I'd eventually implode and cease to exist. Something was off about Vince, I knew it. This story about his grandma's birthday just didn't feel right. Now I needed to know about the money thing as well. My Books were right. I'd been lying to myself when I kept assuming it was just a numbers error I'd made. If Vince's Books were supposedly "right" and he was the only other person with a key to the Tom Petty cashbox, then . . .

I raised my hand. "Mr. Skari, I need to use the restroom."

My teacher scribbled a hall pass, and I was out the door and speed-walking toward my office before I'd even blinked once.

I gathered up Vince's Books as quickly as I could and started going through the most recent transactions. I guess Vince must have thought that I would never take an interest in keeping track of our money, because it didn't take long to notice why everything was off.

Vince had been padding the numbers. According to his Books, we'd paid the bullies slightly more than we actually did. In fact, most all of the recent payments were slightly higher in his Books than they'd actually been. Also, some of the money-received transactions were listed as slightly lower than what we'd taken in.

I was too stunned to breathe. I'm surprised I didn't pass out right there in the office. There had to be some sort of misunderstanding. Vince had always been the money guy. How could this happen? There was only one answer; I just didn't want to admit it. Vince had been padding the numbers so he could steal money undetected. But that didn't make any sense either. Why would Vince do that? This was his business, too, and if he needed extra cash for something, he would come to me and we'd find a way to get it. I couldn't understand why he would possibly be sneaking money like this. I wondered if it had something to do with how weird he'd been acting lately. One thing was for sure—I was going to find out before the day was over.

I slammed his Books shut, surprised at how pissed off I actually was. I put them away and then dug our Tom Petty cashbox out of the garbage can. I hid it inside the empty toilet tank in the second stall. I wasn't just going to sit back and let Vince keep stealing cash until I found out what was going on.

The first thing Vince said when I walked into the office at morning recess was "Mac! Our Tom Petty cash is missing!"

And my first thought was: Why exactly did he look for it first thing when he got here? Answer: He was going to take more money.

"It's not missing," I said.

"What?" Vince asked.

I held out my hand. Vince just looked at it. Joe and Fred walked in, saw us, and instantly stopped talking. I didn't flinch.

"Your Tom Petty key, please," I said, glancing from Vince's face to my open hand.

"Are you serious?" he asked.

"Unless you want to tell me why you've been padding numbers so you can pad your own wallet?"

Vince looked at Fred and Joe and then back at me with a helpless look on his face. I probably should have made sure we would be alone to confront him like this; it would have been the professional thing to do, but right at that moment I didn't really care.

Vince dug the key out of his pocket and handed it to

me without saying anything. No explanation. I suddenly felt like I had just eaten at a seafood buffet that had been sitting out in the hot sun for eight hours. I would wait until later to grill Vince about why he would do such a thing, and why he'd possibly lied to me about his grandma's birthday party being that evening, and what the real reason was he was bailing on us. We had bigger things to take care of just then, like finalizing our plan to take out Justin after school.

"Shall we get down to business, then?" I asked. "Unless of course anybody has any lame jokes they'd like to tell?" I glared at Vince.

He looked away as if he'd just found something really fascinating on the wall that needed his full attention.

Vince didn't talk much the rest of the meeting. Every time I looked at him, he looked away, or put his head down, or rubbed his face. Good. I hoped he felt slimy like a chunk of boiled cabbage. And I was glad he wasn't going to be at the Shed after school. I didn't really want him there anymore anyway. Not if I couldn't trust him. Just thinking that made me want to puke all over my desk.

Chapter 18

I had a hard time thinking about anything but Vince later that day when I met up with Joe, Nubby, Kitten, and Great White outside the Shed. It was thirty minutes before the scheduled meeting with Justin. I tried to put Vince out of my mind. Our plan was dangerous and needed my full attention.

The playground and football field had been deserted since 3:25. Nobody would see what was about to go down. Kids usually cleared out pretty quickly after school and who could blame them? I certainly wasn't going to complain—my plan didn't exactly call for an audience.

I unlocked the Shed with the key I'd snagged from the janitor earlier that day and ushered the bullies inside.

"Blimey, it's bloody hot in here," Great White whined

as they squeezed inside.

"I know. It'll just be twenty minutes, okay?" I said.

"Oh, bollocks to this," he said irritably.

Kitten and Nubby also looked uncomfortable, but they didn't say anything. In fact, I saw Kitten eyeing the tools on the wall like a little kid might the shelves at Toys "R" Us.

I just shrugged and said, "Remember, the signal is 'blue jay.'"

"Just get on with it already," Great White said.

"Okay, see you soon," I said with a grin, and shut the door.

I walked back to the top of the hill overlooking the football field and waited. After about fifteen minutes I saw Justin walking toward the Shed from the far end of the field. There was somebody with him, but I couldn't tell who it was. It looked like I was outnumbered, but Justin didn't know that I had a crew hidden inside the Shed waiting for my signal.

That's why I was surprised to feel so nervous. I was nervous. I couldn't remember the last time I'd felt this kind of anxiety. It must have been way back when I was seven or eight and about to ride my first roller coaster.

Suddenly I really wished that Vince was with me right then, despite everything that had happened that morning. But there wasn't really much I could do about that anymore. So I took a deep breath and trotted down the slope. I slowed at the bottom and walked across the football field to meet up with one of the school's meanest kids. We converged on the Shed at the same time. I nodded. He nodded back. We were about ten feet away from each other, right near the Shed's entrance.

Justin wore really baggy jean shorts with the waist sagging down to his thighs so his boxers showed. I always think it's lame when kids wear their pants so low. It makes them look really dorky, like they just took a dump and forgot to take off their pants first. I also noticed that Justin had shaved his head recently. I wondered if it was some sort of homage to Staples.

The kid with Justin was his best friend, Mitch. The two are always together. And they are usually up to no good, like cheating, skipping school, smoking, or beating up younger kids, either for money or just because they feel like it. They're basically a walking-talking duo of terror.

Mitch also wore baggy jean shorts and a black T-shirt. His head wasn't shaved, though; instead he was sporting his usual greasy brown hair and a white, straight-brimmed New York Yankees baseball hat worn slightly off to the side. He had his hands behind his back. I didn't like that, but in just a few moments it wouldn't matter.

"Thanks for coming," I said.

"Whatever, man, just say what you gotta say," Justin said.

At that moment I saw Mitch take three quick steps toward the Shed. His hands came out from around his back to reveal a bike lock. The kind that is like a big U shape with a little bar that locks on to the end. I knew immediately what he was going to do with it.

"Blue jay!" I shouted as loud as I could.

But it was too late. Mitch slid the bike lock into the Shed's door handles and then snapped on the lock bar. The doors clanked as the bullies and Joe tried to jump out. But the lock was in place, and the doors clattered harmlessly against themselves, the bullies yelling from inside.

Mitch and Justin laughed at their pleas.

"Trying to pull a fast one on me?" Justin scoffed.

My stomach sank. I had been double-crossed. They knew. They had known everything about our plan. The worst part was that the Shed was like a sauna inside, and now the bullies and Joe would be trapped in there for who knew how long.

The natural thing to do at that point would probably have been to run. But I couldn't leave behind my hired muscle to cook like that—it wouldn't be right. Besides, there were only two of them; maybe I could still get us out of this.

But that's when the chunky ham and fish-head gravy really hit the fan, as Vince's grandma says. A car squealed to a stop behind me. I turned around and saw a black Honda with a spoiler so huge the car could probably have taken flight if it was going fast enough. The four high school kids from last Tuesday clamored out of the car and walked toward me, with PJ in the lead.

"Well, well, well, if it isn't Mr. Problem Solver Guy," PJ said. "How nice to see you again."

I just looked at him right in the eyes and said nothing, trying to stay calm.

"Oooh, looks like we got a tough guy on our hands, boys," PJ said with a sickening grin.

The four high school kids, Justin, and Mitch grouped around me in a circle. Their shadows blocked out what little sunlight there was that day.

"You won't be so tough after we're finished with you," PJ said.

I knew that my only chance of survival was to strike first. To surprise them. I wasn't much of a fighter; in fact, I'd never gotten into a real fight before. But I figured I was smarter than all of these guys combined and that gave me at least one advantage.

I spun around as they enveloped me. I quickly determined PJ to be the closest, and one of the high school kids with greasy black hair to be the biggest.

"Hey, let's talk about this, guys. I've got money. I'll pay you. I can double what you're making now."

PJ scoffed.

"I doubt it," Justin said.

"Right here in my pocket I have a roll of money, and I have even more in my office." I reached into the pocket of my jeans.

They leaned forward eagerly. All that was in my pocket was the note I had sent to Justin. I grabbed it and pulled it out. But as my hand cleared my pocket I let the paper flutter to the grass. I made a motion like I wanted to pick it back up.

PJ predictably bent over to get it first. That's when I struck at him with my foot. I didn't really have a clear plan, because like I said, I'm not a fighter. But in this case it was them or me.

I quickly kicked back the same foot so my heel slammed into the shin of the big greasy high schooler behind me. I heard him hit the ground with a grunt. Then I turned and kicked another kid in the knee. He hit the ground like dead weight.

The high school kid to my right reached out for me. I spun to face him and took a step back to avoid his reach. Two big hands grabbed my arms from behind. I had stepped right into them.

I swung my body from side to side, trying to free

myself, but the hands were too strong and the fingers just dug into my arms even harder. By now another kid was coming at me from the front. He had a huge smile on his face as he cracked his knuckles. I was a sitting duck and he knew it.

"Let's see what you got, loser," I said.

"Okay," he said, and reared back his fist.

That's when I leaned back into the kid holding me and kicked my leg up as hard as I could. My foot connected with the one spot sure to cause the most damage. I'd never wish that sort of pain upon anyone, but this was life or death.

"OOOoh," he moaned as he crossed his legs and dropped to the ground.

The kid holding my arms actually snickered. I guess it's normally pretty funny when people get hit in the groin. Now it was his turn, though. I stamped my heel into his shin as hard as I could. He yelled and his grip loosened. I pulled away from him, and then turned and gave him my best shot. He dropped to the ground and started crying. I almost felt bad.

PJ was still down holding his face, two other kids were in the fetal position holding their "business," and another one was trying to get to his feet again. I looked at Justin, the only one still standing. He looked scared.

I walked toward him, but then I stopped when I heard loud banging on the Shed.

PJ had gotten up and was standing next to the doors. He held a small black tube in his hand like a can of hair spray. He stuck it against the crevice of the Shed's doors.

"Stop fighting, Mac, or I'll douse your little friends," he said.

There could have been anything inside that black tube. It could have just been water. I looked around as the other kids were climbing back to their feet. It wasn't a risk I was willing to take with my employees trapped inside.

"Okay," I said, holding my hands up.

All of my confidence just drained out of me like ice cream from the little hole in the bottom of a waffle cone on a hot day. The other high school kids were on their feet now. Two of them grabbed me, one on each side. They squeezed hard and I felt a pain shoot through my arms. I was surrounded by kids, but I'd never felt so alone in my life.

"You're in trouble now, you little punk," one of them said.

I wanted to say "Duh," but I thought it best to stay quiet right then.

Mitch, PJ, and Justin closed in on me. PJ used his Hollister shirt to wipe his face. His nose was red. I hoped I hadn't broken it.

"You're going to pay for this," he said, looking down at his shirt.

I nodded while raising my eyebrows and said, "Yup."

"Are you smarting off to me?" PJ yelled.

I nodded.

That's when sharp pain erupted in my stomach. I hadn't even seen it coming. I always thought that people overreact in movies when they get hit in the gut. I mean, how bad could it hurt, right? Well, I can say that it hurts way worse than it looks.

The air shot out of me and a sharp pain stabbed my stomach, followed by a deep rumble that ran straight to my brain. I gasped for air, trying not to cry. It hurt worse than I ever would have imagined it could. I tried to bend over, but the two high school kids held me up. I wheezed for air, sure I was going to suffocate.

PJ laughed.

"Not such a cocky punk now?"

The other kids laughed. One holding my arm whispered into my ear, "It's payback time."

I continued to struggle to breathe. Just when I thought it was all over, that I was going to pass out, I finally was able to get some air in. But that's when the side of my face exploded. Okay, it probably didn't explode, but that's what it felt like.

It basically felt like Barry Bonds took batting practice on my head with a titanium baseball bat. My vision blurred and my eyes watered. I tasted blood in my mouth.

I think I'll spare you the rest—it wasn't too pretty. They worked me over for what seemed like a couple hours. It couldn't have been that long; when they stopped it was still pretty light out. I was proud that I never cried, but toward the middle I just started to go numb. I think maybe they broke my tear ducts or something, because it hurt so bad I definitely should have been crying.

I kept wondering the whole time why no cars were stopping to help me. Maybe they just didn't notice the little kid getting the snot beat out of him by a gang of high schoolers? Maybe they were too afraid to stop? Or just didn't care? Or maybe they were all on Staples's payroll, too? In any event, Staples's hit men eventually dropped me onto the ground. I looked up to see PJ looming over me with a big smile.

"That's for Barnaby. And there's a lot more where that came from. Slow and painful, just like Staples said, right, Mac?" They all walked away laughing.

After a while I climbed to my feet. My stomach ached and my side hurt and my face felt like a lumpy piece of deep-fried cheese. I spit some blood onto the grass and gently touched my cheek. I winced. My whole face throbbed. I was relieved to find that I at least had all of my teeth.

The Shed burst open about that time. Mitch must have taken the bike lock with him when he left. Kitten emerged, soaked in sweat. He stumbled forward a few feet and then sat down. He breathed hard, his sweater and collared shirt were soggy, and his normally neat hair stuck up all over.

Nubby, Great White, and Joe followed. Their clothes were drenched and they panted as if they'd just run a marathon. We had just gotten wasted. Mitch and Justin had known everything. It had been a classic double ambush.

"Mac, I can hardly breathe," Joe said.

I nodded and pointed to a spigot behind the Shed.

The four of them took turns drinking from it. After a few more minutes of walking around and breathing hard and taking off their drenched shirts and wringing out all the sweat, they looked a little better.

"Wow, Mac, what did they do to you?" Joe asked after examining my face.

"I'm okay. They were just sending me a little message. Don't worry about it," I said.

He shook his head and whistled.

"They're not getting away with this," Kitten said softly.

His eyes were beady and dark. His mouth was drawn into a tight frown. I'd seen that look before. Kitten was angry. The insane little kid looked like he wanted to grab a shovel from the Shed and beat someone's face in with it. And he would have, too, had the enemy still been there.

"Aye. Those wankers will pay. I'll kick their arses," Great White added.

"We will, guys. We'll get back at them," I said. "For now, though, you should all just go home. If you want to stay on board and help me get back at these jerks, meet me in my office tomorrow at morning recess."

They nodded. With that, we all parted ways to go home. The walk felt much longer than nine or ten blocks. I couldn't think about anything but who had double-crossed us. One person kept creeping into my mind as the obvious suspect, but I kept erasing it immediately. Because there was no way. Skimming some cash was one thing, but double-crossing your best friend into that kind of beating? No. There was no way he'd do that.

Whoever the snitch was, though, we needed to figure it out, and fast.

Chapter 19

Vince was waiting for me in my room when I got home.

"What happened?" Vince asked as he examined my face.

I had told my parents that I hurt it while doing some crazy stunt on my bike. It's the same story I told every time I got an injury. They always believed it. They must have thought I was the worst bike rider in the world. That's one thing I've learned from watching reality TV shows: When you're lying, consistency is important. You can't always be changing your story or no one will believe you.

I didn't say anything to Vince. I could barely stand to look at him.

"Mac, I'm sorry. I really am. I should have told you," Vince started.

"Told me what? That you were *stealing* money? Yeah, I guess that would have been nice to know!"

Vince sighed. "Mac, please just hear me out, okay? I was too embarrassed to say anything today with Fred and Joe there, but I've got a reason. Will you please just hear me out?"

"Fine," I said. It'd better be good, I thought, or this is going to be a solo operation from now on.

"It's my mom. She lost her job a few weeks ago. And, well, we're not like your family, Mac. We don't have a house and cars, and I don't have a dad making any money to help out. My mom hasn't been able to find another job, and she's been sitting around the house in her robe all day talking to the TV. I mean, when my grandma does stuff like that it's funny, but with Mom it's just freaking me out," he said. He was close to tears now, and already some guilt was starting to creep in and replace my anger.

I nodded at him to continue.

"We're in bad shape, and my brother has been giving part of his paychecks to her, which has been making her embarrassed, but she still takes it because we're that desperate. So I've been helping out where I can. I mean, I'm not giving her the cash personally, because she'd never take it from me, but I've been slipping twenties into her purse when she's sleeping and stuff like that, and I think she just doesn't question where it comes from. Once I even heard her thanking my dad one night when she found a ten that I'd put in her dresser drawer. But either way, it's been making a difference. I mean, how could I sit back and let us lose our trailer or have our heat and water cut off when I know what kind of money we're sitting on?"

I nodded again. "You could've just come to me for help. You didn't have to steal it . . . ."

"Well, that's easy for you to say, isn't it? You don't know what it's like to have breakfast for dinner four nights a week because pancakes are cheap. Or to get Victor's old clothes as birthday presents. I was embarrassed, Mac. It's embarrassing."

He was right. I didn't really know what that's like. My family had moved out of that trailer park years ago. I barely remember what it's like not to get new presents for birthdays and holidays and not to get to go on vacations to Disney World and stuff like that. I sometimes forget that Vince still lives in that same old yellow-and-red trailer with brown carpet that always smells like milk for some reason. This actually explained a lot. It also explained why he'd been acting so miserly lately about hiring kids to help Fred.

"I'm sorry, Vince. You're right. But you should know you don't have to be embarrassed. You're my best friend, my business partner. I've got your back no matter what. We could've worked something out."

He nodded. "I guess. But I was also worried about the Cubs game. I couldn't take it if we missed it because of my crazy mom. I mean, if I ruined that for us, I'd probably have to denounce my Cubs fandom forever and declare you the better fan, which we both know isn't true. I mean, it can't be, considering how much more Cubs trivia I know."

I looked at him and a grin slowly spread across his face. Then I burst out laughing, which hurt my sore cheeks. "Ow," I said, rubbing my face.

"I'm sorry, Mac. I should have come to you. That's also why I missed our ambush today. My mom had this job interview, and she needed me to watch my little sister because Victor had to work and she can't afford our usual babysitter anymore. Speaking of which, what happened? I mean, judging from your face . . ."

"They knew, Vince. They knew about the plan. I got beat up, and the bullies and Joe all got trapped in the Shed and baked to a crisp inside that huge tin oven. We were ambushed."

Vince couldn't even speak. We sat there for a while just staring at our own sections of the floor.

"Are you guys okay?" Vince finally said.

"What do you think?" I said a little harsher than I'd intended.

"Sorry, Mac, I didn't mean . . ." Vince started.

"My face hurts, that's all, and it's making me edgy. The bullies are fine and I'll live. Probably."

I still didn't feel all that bad for snapping at him, though. I mean, yeah his mom had lost her job and that sucked, but he'd still gotten to avoid the ambush. A fact that still had me feeling a little uneasy, despite believing, deep down, that Vince would never betray me.

"I should have been there!" Vince said.

"If you'd have been there, then you would have just gotten beat up, too. You really think you could have taken them all out on your own? The guy who avoids confrontations like they're the plague?" I asked.

He didn't say anything for second and then said, "Yeah. Of course."

I almost laughed.

"Mac, you know what this means then, right?" he said.

"That we've been double-crossed. Again," I said.

"We have a traitor amongst us," he said. "It's like Benedict Arnold all over again."

"Who?"

"Never mind," Vince said. "Look, we need to figure out who it is. For Justin to know about this plan . . . it would have to be one of us. Someone actually involved with the plan sold us out. We've been had, Mac."

"You know, they're all going to think it's you, Vince. I

mean, they just got wasted and you conveniently missed the whole thing just after getting caught stealing money. It looks pretty suspicious."

Vince's face turned red and he looked away.

We both sat in silence as I started pacing my room.

"This is just like Pearl Harbor. If only we'd listened to the warnings!" Vince said.

"What? Pearl Harbor? Vince, stop talking like a freaking historian and come up with an actual idea that will help us!" Vince had never in my life annoyed me so much.

"Sorry, Mac, I'm trying," he said.

"Whatever," I said.

We sat uncomfortably in an awkward silence for a while, as if we were both wearing itchy wool bodysuits in one-hundred-degree weather. I didn't feel like I really had anything more I wanted to say to Vince right then, but then I remembered what kind of mess he had to go home to and I decided to send him off feeling a little better.

"Okay, Mr. Chicago Cub, here's a real test for you: Who was the first Cub to win a Cy Young?" I said, tossing him a floater.

"Fergie Jenkins," Vince said. After a pause he added, "I'm sorry, Mac."

"I'll see you tomorrow, okay?" I said.

He nodded and left.

• • •

"Someone snitched," I said calmly. "We've been two-timed. Backstabbed. Double-crossed. Ratted out. Sold up the river. We're not moving forward until we find out who it is."

We were all sitting in the East Wing boys' bathroom: Fred, Joe, Vince, the three bullies, and I. It was Wednesday, the day after the ambush. I had just finished explaining to Fred what had happened to our plan, how it had been turned upside down.

"But who?" Fred nearly screeched.

A silence followed as we all looked at one another. Nobody flinched. It seemed like nobody breathed. It was kind of like a seven-way staring contest. I looked at Great White the most. He looked really angry. He was staring at Vince. Nubby was also glaring at Vince. In fact, *everybody* seemed to be staring at Vince.

I myself was feeling pretty conflicted about Vince. Up to now most of the evidence did seem to point at him. And while I remained convinced he'd never do something like this to me, if you'd told me two days ago that he would steal money from me, I'd have slapped you in the face with a spiral-bound notebook and called you a dirty liar. So *anything* was possible.

"Look," I said, breaking the silence, "we can't just sit here accusing each other. I need some time to think, so let's just plan on meeting here again tomorrow at morning recess, okay?"

Everybody was pretty quiet. Finally Nubby said, "Okay."

"Just use your day off to relax, all right?" I said to everybody.

With that, the three bullies left the bathroom. I asked Joe, Vince, and Fred to stay for a moment.

"I want to call a private meeting just for us," I said to them, "but it's not safe here. We're already going to my house right after school to help my dad clean off the graffiti, so we'll hold our meeting after we're done."

"I just need to call my mom and let her know that I'll be home a little later than usual," Fred said.

Fred had been there the day I told Joe and Vince about the graffiti and my dad's offer. Fred insisted that he be allowed to help. He blamed himself for the graffiti, so he felt he owed it to me to help clean it off. And, well, it kind of *was* his fault.

"Let's close the office for the rest of the day. I'll see you guys after school," I said.

For the first time in my life I was really happy to be going to class. Schoolwork just seemed so simple and easy compared to the mess I was in with the business. I watched the other kids working. They had the easy life. No money or business worries. No Staples. If they only knew how good they had it, they wouldn't complain so much about having homework and lame assignments and everything else like that.

At lunch that day it was time to put my own private plan into action. I picked my way through the different groups and cliques of kids, working my way across the north baseball field and over to the little Dumpster on the far side of the school parking lot. It's a pretty private place, and kids are not usually allowed back there, but like I said before about the recess supervisor: She doesn't like walking much.

I found my target sitting against the Dumpster reading a book. Just where I knew he'd be. Tyrell Alishouse, über–spy extraordinaire, looked up at me.

"Oh hey, Mac," he said.

I nodded at him and said, "Hey."

Whenever sleuthing or sneaking had to be done, Tyrell is my guy. Ever since his brilliant exposure of the Graffiti Ninja, he has been my number one spy. And he loves spying on people, so he's always willing to help. Honestly, I should have gone to him sooner. Maybe I could have avoided this mess. But his services are expensive and I just didn't think it was necessary, especially with the way Vince had been acting about our shrinking piles of cash. Now I just couldn't take any more chances. I needed the truth even if it meant breaking the bank to get it.

"What's up?" he asked, putting his book aside. It was

called *The Spycraft Manual.*

"I need your help. People who I need monitored."

"Oh really?" he asked with a smile.

I nodded.

"What sort of monitoring?"

"I need you to follow some people and let me know what they're up to, who they're spending time with. Basically, I need to know if any of my friends and employees have decided to switch sides."

"Interesting. That sounds like some pretty extensive monitoring. Possibly dangerous, too. It might cost you," he said.

"This I know," I said.

He nodded and looked at the ground. I could tell he was just bursting with excitement. He loved challenges, especially dangerous ones. And this was the biggest I'd sent his way perhaps since the case of the Graffiti Ninja.

"What's the offer?" he asked, looking up at me.

"I'll double your usual fee. Half now, half once you get me some hard information."

Tyrell pretended to ponder the offer for a while. He would accept; he always does.

"Consider it done," he finally said. "So who exactly am I shadowing this time?"

I sat down next to him, took a deep breath, and began talking.

Chapter 20

"Oh, you're so dead now," Joe said as he cornered me.

"No, come on. I can't believe it!" I yelled.

I tried to run, but I was stuck in the corner. There was nowhere to go. I lifted my own weapon, but it was no use. It was empty.

"Good-bye, sucker," he said, and pulled the trigger of his Uzi.

He had tricked me and I paid for it with my life.

Fred and Vince laughed. Then Joe and I joined in. We were all sitting in my bedroom playing video games, having just finished helping my dad clean off the graffiti. Which had been a lot of work. The spray paint wouldn't wash off, so we had to repaint over it completely. Now we were just killing some time while my dad ran out to get us a movie and my mom baked us cookies. I wanted to hold the meeting in the basement with the movie going as a cover.

"I'm going to sit this one out," I said, getting up.

Fred, Joe, and Vince started another round. They were pretty focused on the game so it seemed like a good time to get something from my closet. I went to the back corner and removed the loose wood paneling. I took out the first half of Tyrell's fee from the Emergency Fund and put the wood panel back.

"Oh, shoot. Fred, you sneaky little punk!" Vince yelled.

I peeked out of the closet and looked at the screen. Fred had just sniped Vince's guy from the old church tower. Fred always used the sniper strategy. He was pretty good for a third grader.

After they finished their game, I turned off the machine.

"It's time," I said.

They reluctantly agreed. None of us wanted to face the truth: There was a snitch among us, and we had to find out who it was.

We all went down to the basement, where my mom had milk, soda, chips, and fresh-baked chocolate chip cookies waiting for us. My dad had rented us some action movie to watch. It was a reward for helping him clean off the house. He also gave each of my friends five bucks.

"Oh, you guys are so cute," my mom squealed as we came down the stairs to the basement.

"Mom!" I said.

"Oh, Christian, relax. I just think it's great that you're having Fred over. I spoke to his mom earlier and she is just thrilled that he found some new friends. You boys enjoy your movie."

"Mom! Please?" She could be so embarrassing.

"Okay, okay," she said, heading for the stairs.

"Thank you for the cookies, Mrs. Barrett," Vince said.

She smiled at him and went upstairs.

"Dude, your mom is cool. My mom would never make me and my friends cookies," Joe said.

"Yeah, I know, whatever," I said.

"Just wait till you're fourteen, like me. Then she'll be nagging you all the time to clean your room or take out the trash or not to slouch or chew with your mouth open or to say thank you and 'don't be disrespectful' and 'call me and let me know where you're going' and blah, blah, blah, blah. Dude, you'll miss the days when she makes you snacks and stuff." Joe bit into one of the cookies.

"Okay, okay, let's just get down to business," I said, turning on the TV.

I hit Play and turned up the volume. The movie had lots of explosions and guys rolling around shooting huge guns and lots of slow-motion shots of bullets zooming around. It looked pretty good. But we weren't there to watch it.

"Okay, the reason I wanted to hold this meeting is because we need to figure out who the rat is."

We all brainstormed for a while and tossed around name after name. We didn't really get anywhere, especially since Joe and Vince were afraid to accuse each other since they were both sitting right there. But it didn't matter to me; this meeting was just a cover to distract everybody while Tyrell did his thing.

"Now then, I guess for the time being we should just lay low, let things cool off before we make our next move." It had been a half hour of pointless speculation.

They all nodded whether they agreed or not, and either way I didn't care.

I felt really bad lying to them all. It wasn't like me. But I just needed some time to execute my own plan, to let Tyrell do what he does best. I needed to get to the bottom of this, and I didn't know who to trust anymore.

After our discussion we all settled in and tried to watch the movie and have some fun. My face was starting to throb again, but I didn't want to ask my mom for more Tylenol because then she would bother us. So I just ate some cookies and tried to distract myself with the explosions and whatnot.

Toward the end of the movie I saw Fred look down at his watch. He jumped up.

"Oh man! I gotta go now. My mom said she'd pick me up at seven and it's seven oh five. See you guys later."

"Yeah, I better go, too," Joe said. "I told my friend David that I would hang out with him tonight. I've been so busy lately that we haven't hung out much."

"All right, see you tomorrow at morning recess," I said.

Vince nodded good-bye and then Joe left. I sometimes forgot that Joe just worked for me. We weren't his best friends or anything.

So then it was just Vince and I. We switched it to the Cubs play-off game at 7:15. The best moment of the game was when the Cubs executed a perfect suicide squeeze play. Vince jumped up and yelled and screamed like they'd just won the World Series. He loved the suicide squeeze. If you let him, he would ramble on for hours about how amazing and beautiful it was to watch one perfectly executed.

"That was the best; did you see that bunt?" Vince asked as he sat back down.

"Yeah, that was a good one," I said. "I was just thinking about how amazing it'd be to be at Wrigley to see the

Cubs pull off a squeeze in a World Series game."

Vince shuddered and his smile disappeared.

"It's almost cruel to hope for something so amazing. I'm so excited for the Cubs trip right now it's like I'm in a reverse coma—a constant state of hyperactivity. Or as my grandma might say, 'Don't wash the cat until the raccoon eats his glue stick.'"

I just shook my head at him. I didn't really get the impression that he *was* all that excited. Sure, he'd been acting extra cheery all night, but it was like he was just pretending that I hadn't caught him stealing money and lying to me.

"Anyways, I just thought of a good one: Who was the first manager to win the World Series for the Cubs?" Vince asked.

"Come on, Vince. Don't you remember that I'm obsessed with Cubs World Series trivia? It was Frank Chance, and they beat the Detroit Tigers. And I'll even go ahead and say that their final record was one hundred seven wins, forty-five losses and that you should try a little harder next time," I said.

"Careful what you ask for, Mac," Vince said with a cheesy smile.

"Okay, whatever," I said.

We watched the game in silence for a few minutes.

"Do you think it's Great White?" Vince asked suddenly.

"I don't know. We'll just have to wait and see, I guess. If it is him, he'll slip up eventually."

I was careful not to sound too complacent. I still felt bad about keeping my Tyrell plan from him, but that's what this had come to.

After the game we watched Cartoon Network for a little bit. Some show was on about a box of French fries, a meatball, and a milk shake who all talked and fought crime. We didn't talk much, which wasn't like us at all.

"I think I'd better go," Vince said after the show.

"Oh okay. I'll see you tomorrow then, right?" I said.

"Sure."

He headed upstairs and I heard the front door open and close a few moments later. After he left, I realized something that bothered me so badly, I barely slept that night. Together that night we'd watched the Cubs win a play-off game to take a commanding 2–0 lead over the Phillies in the NLCS, but it had felt more like we were watching a funeral. The Cubs almost never made the play-offs. This was the first time they'd made it this far in our lives. And usually when we watched even a regular-season Cubs game together, there was yelling and shouting and cursing and then we'd both do a really horrible job singing "Go Cubs Go" with the crowd on TV when they won. But that night, other than after the suicide squeeze the Cubs had pulled off early in the game, we'd basically just sat there and watched like zombies. It became very clear to me right then that there was a whole lot more falling apart than just our business.

The first sign that something was seriously wrong the next day was that Vince didn't come to school. I wasn't sure exactly what that meant, but I knew it probably wasn't good. And as much as I wished I was wrong about that, what unfolded the rest of the day proved me to be more right than I'd ever wanted to be before.

It started during morning recess. I was sitting in my office with my face in my hands trying to figure out just where everything had gone wrong. How had I gotten myself mixed up in this mess?

Eventually I looked up.

"Holy . . . ! Are you trying to give me a heart attack?" I yelled.

"Sorry, Mac," Tyrell said.

He was seated across from me in my office. The kid is amazing. I had no idea how he got inside the office and into the chair without Joe, Fred, or me noticing. I guess that's why he's the best.

"It's okay. It's what you do, I guess. So what's up?"

"I have information for you," he said.

"Already?"

"I work fast, Mac. You know that."

I nodded. I guess I did know that. He is a darn fine spy.

"What did you find?"

"Okay, Mac. You're really not going to like what I found. It's pretty shocking," he said.

I nodded and motioned for him to continue. What could be more shocking at this point than finding out you have a mole on the inside selling you out and that your best friend has been stealing money?

"Well, everybody you asked me to monitor has checked out so far with no suspicious activity or unusual affiliations. Except for one person."

I had a bad feeling about this. I had really expected him to say Joe. Or maybe that's just what I wanted him to say. Not that I would've liked hearing that, but Joe was the only one who made sense anymore.

"Who is it?" I asked warily.

"It's Vince," he said. My heart started thumping against the inside of my rib cage as if it was trying to bust out of jail. "Now, it might not mean anything, but I caught him conversing with a person of interest."

"Who?" I asked.

Tyrell started digging in his bag while shaking his head. "I'm not really sure. I've got my theories, but I've never actually seen this kid before. Why don't you take a look first?" He took a little video camera the size of a deck of cards from his canvas messenger bag and laid it on my desk. "Hit Play."

"Wow, this is really clear," I said.

"It's the *Rear Window* Edition P-Tom that I got for my birthday."

The video was zoomed in pretty close so it would have been hard to tell exactly where the footage was taking place had I not been there myself at least a thousand times before. It was the playground near Vince's trailer. It was the very same playground in which Vince and I had first started our business. Now it was pretty rundown. The sandbox was a dirt-and-weed box. Only one seat actually remained on the swing set, and it creaked and croaked like a ten-pack-a-day lunch lady asking you for your lunch card. But the playground was still unmistakable.

I also recognized the kid talking to Vince near the old playground slide right away, despite the baseball hat sitting on top of his shaved head. I would never forget that face for the rest of my life. It was Staples.

The video footage on the little screen showed Vince standing with his back to the rusted slide. Staples stood close to him, and appeared to be the one doing most of the talking. At the end Staples held out what looked to be a roll of cash. Vince looked hesitant, but then finally he reached out and took the money. The last bit showed Staples walking away with a grin on his face and Vince standing at the slide until well after Staples had left. Then Vince stuffed the money into his pocket and walked into his trailer.

"When was this taken?" I asked, my voice coming out cracked and broken like a scratched CD.

"This morning around six forty-five," Tyrell said.

That would be right around the time Vince would be leaving for school. So had Staples paid him to skip school today? If so, why? Or had the payment been for something else?

"How did it all play out?" I asked.

"Well, he left his trailer that morning and headed for his bike. And that's when the kid in the baseball hat approached him and pulled him aside toward the slide. They spent the next few minutes talking there. Sorry, Mac, but I couldn't really get close enough to hear what they said. That's a pretty open place."

"That's okay, Tyrell. You did well," I said, and slid part of his payment across my desk. He grabbed it, and almost before I could blink, he was gone.

So Staples visits with Vince this morning and then he's coincidentally gone today? And he doesn't even bother to call and tell me that Staples approached him? Or maybe he did call me. I couldn't be sure because I'd already left my house by 6:45 this morning. It could have been nothing, and it certainly didn't prove anything definite, but it didn't look very good either. In fact, it looked downright horrible.

I doubled over my desk and banged my forehead on its surface.

"You okay?" Fred called out from his chair in the corner near the first stall.

I couldn't even muster a response. This couldn't possibly mean what it looked like, could it? There was no way Vince was on Staples's payroll. No way. But what if he was? And if that was true, then what exactly was he doing right now instead of coming to school? And what had the money been for? Was I really this big of a sucker?

Chapter 21

At lunch that day I broke a school rule that came with a mandatory three-day in-school suspension if caught. But I didn't care. This was bigger than a suspension now; it probably always had been, if my hunch was right. And I needed to know immediately if I was right. I just hoped I was wrong.

I had Joe close up the office and then I snuck around to the front of the school and got my bike. Joe arranged for a distraction to keep the RS on the other side of the school until I could get clear.

I stayed low and walked my bike to the edge of the parking lot, and then I was off. I pedaled toward home as fast as I could. My butt never even touched the seat, and I made the usual seven-minute bike ride in three minutes. My mom's car was not in the garage. She must have had to work. Her work schedule was pretty irregular, so I never knew when she did or didn't work.

The front and side doors were locked and I didn't have my key. In my haste, I'd left it in my backpack at the school. I cursed myself for being so stupid as I jogged around to the back of the house. I climbed the tree in our backyard and clambered onto the roof. This is how Vince used to come up to my room until my dad yelled at me once and said Vince could just use the darn front door like a normal person. Except he hadn't said darn. Even still, I always left my window open in case Vince needed to drop by unexpectedly in the middle of the night or something.

I crawled across the roof to my bedroom window and noticed right away that it was ajar about an inch. My heart sank. No. No, he wouldn't do that.

I opened the window and climbed through it. My shoes felt like they were made of lead. I could barely walk and I almost fell once I was actually inside my room. I opened my closet and knelt next to the false wood panel. I popped it off, set it aside, and reached into the hole.

There was nothing. I reached up and down and all around, but all I felt was dusty insulation and particleboard. My heart caught in my throat and I couldn't swallow.

I scrambled up to my desk and took a flashlight from the top drawer. I went back to the cubbyhole in my closet and got down on my stomach. I shined the light inside. I made a pass over every corner and space that I could find. But all I saw was dust that moved in the flashlight's yellow beam. There was no mistake about it: The Emergency Fund and the Game Fund had been stolen. Around six thousand dollars was just gone as if it had never even existed. I resisted the urge to puke. The Cubs games, our business, our money, everything I had worked so hard for my whole life was gone in the blink of an eye. And it was probably my best friend who had done it.

I got up and ran to the bathroom, where I puked out my Cinnamon Toast Crunch, my guts, and, I think, my heart, from the feel of it.

I still didn't want to believe it. It felt like someone had just burned down my house with my family still inside and now the arsonist was laughing at me and making snow angels in the ashes. During the bike ride back to school I went over it all again, sure I had missed some key detail that would prove I was crazy and had imagined it all. But it always came back to the same end result. Staples had paid off Vince, and Vince had stolen our Funds. That's what their meeting had been about this morning; I was sure of it. It explained why Vince had been acting so weird lately.

That's also why Vince had not gone to school today. So he could sneak into my room and steal my money. He was the only person who knew where it was hidden besides Fred and Joe, and they had both been at school all day, and the money had been there when I'd left that morning. I knew because I'd checked. I always do—it's a morning ritual for me. Vince also had had plenty of practice climbing into my bedroom through my unlocked window.

I knew I would have to confront Vince about it all at some point. Or maybe I would order a hit on him. A hit on my own best friend. I didn't really like the thought of either of those options.

But then I realized that it didn't matter. As I arrived back at school, the truth really set in. My Empire had officially crumbled. I had nothing left at all. All of my money was gone. Joe would probably abandon me once he found out. The bullies wouldn't work for free. I had no way to pay Tyrell what I owed him. What was left in Tom Petty cash wouldn't be nearly enough. And it was Vince, my supposed best friend in the world and business manager, who had taken me down, so I didn't even have anyone to brainstorm with or talk to. I was alone and my business was all but gone.

Staples had been right. He had dismantled my whole life and I never saw it coming. And that's why he knew he'd be successful, because he had my right-hand man in his back pocket the entire time. I had been doomed from the start. I could still hardly believe it. The whole thing hurt much worse than the beating PJ and the high schoolers had laid on me a few days before. It hurt on a whole different level. That had been just a pinprick compared to this.

As I trudged back to class, I couldn't help but wonder. Maybe I should have just gone to work for Staples? Then Vince and I would still be friends and business partners. We'd still probably be going to the Cubs games. People like Staples never seemed to have these problems. Maybe that was the answer after all.

I tried to pay attention in class that day, but it was no use. I didn't really listen to Mr. Skari talking about compounded fractoids or whatever he was babbling on about. And I definitely didn't write down the assignment or care in the least about trying to work on it. All I could think about was Vince and our business and how it used to be way back in that trailer park sandbox. Those days had never seemed so far away.

But maybe this was partially my fault. Why else would my best friend betray me like this? Vince had finally fessed up to stealing money, and it had been because his family was in desperate need. And sure, I'd forgiven him, but what else had I done? Nothing. I could have offered him some more money, but I didn't. And Staples clearly had, and that had been the difference. Staples had offered Vince what he needed more than anything and I didn't. Had I really driven Vince to this in some way?

At afternoon recess I met with Joe, Kitten, Great White, Nubby, and Fred. The mood was somber and I think they could tell that something was wrong. It was time to tell them that I had found the traitor. I wasn't going to say exactly who it was yet, because I thought I should deal with Vince personally first. He was my former best friend, and it was that friendship that had blinded *me* from the double cross. My belief in my friend had doomed us all. It was my responsibility to deal with Vince, not theirs.

I also decided to not tell them just yet about my lack of funds either. The longer I could keep them on my side, the better. Though I would obviously have to come clean at some point.

"I think I've found our rat," I said.

"Who is it? I'll kick his bloody arse!" Great White said.

"If you all meet me here tomorrow morning, I'll

discuss it then. I just wanted to let you all know that we can stop being suspicious of each other. And you should all take the rest of the day off. Go be kids. Have fun. I'll see you all here tomorrow morning at recess. And Joe?" I added as they filed out.

"Yeah, Mac?"

"Make sure you stick pretty close to Fred. Staples may still be gunning for him."

"Okay, sure."

I watched Fred and Joe exit together. They looked like a pretty funny pair. I would have laughed had the circumstances been different.

I sat inside my office, not even bothering to lock the bathroom door. Why should I care anymore? My customers had all pretty much given up on my business; hardly anybody lined up outside the bathroom anymore, even when my office was open. I thought word had started to spread about what Staples had been doing to me. The assault outside the Shed, my inability to protect my hired bullies . . . I was losing my cred. But who cared about that stuff? I had no partner anymore, no best friend. And I had no money because my greedy former best friend had stolen it.

After a few minutes I buried my face in my hands and tried not to think too much about Vince. My stomach and chest hurt like I'd just drunk a huge bottle of acid.

• • •

The bike ride to Vince's house after school was hard. And it took forever even though it was just under a few miles or so. Most likely it was because I really didn't want to have to face Vince. Not after everything that had happened.

It seemed like I was never going to make it, but eventually I rounded the corner onto his block. I parked my bike and walked down the leaf-littered path up to Vince's trailer. My stomach churned in anticipation as I knocked on his door. I still had no idea what even to say to him. There was so much going on inside my head that I didn't even notice that Vince's mom had answered.

"Christian, dear, are you okay?" she said loudly.

"Oh, sorry. I was just thinking."

"I thought you had heat stroke. Get in here," she demanded, and stepped aside for me. I noticed that she was wearing sweatpants and a sweatshirt and looked as if she hadn't showered in days.

Vince's mom was such a riot. She usually made me laugh. Not today, though; nothing could make me laugh today. Betrayal can do that to a person.

"Vince is in his room. He's not feeling well today," she said with a smile.

"Thanks," I said, and went down the hall toward his room.

Not feeling well because stabbing his best friend in the back made him feel horrible? Probably not. He probably just ate too much during his celebration lunch with Staples.

My forced smile quickly faded as I approached Vince's door. It was closed and his "If *I* don't know why you're here, then why *are* you here?" sign was hanging on the outside. I remembered giving him that sign for his ninth birthday. I walked up to the door, took a breath, tried to clear my mind, and knocked.

"Come in," came Vince's voice.

I opened the door and stepped inside. He smiled like nothing was wrong.

"What's up, Mac?" he said.

"Vince, we need to talk." I closed the door behind me.

He sat on his bed wearing sweatpants and a T-shirt. His hair was sticking up everywhere as if he hadn't left the trailer at all today, but I knew better.

"Anything you want to tell me?" I asked.

He narrowed his eyes, and then smiled. "Uh, yeah, I guess about not making it to school today . . . I'd meant to call you but it was—"

"It was what?" I interrupted. "Too hard to face your best friend after stabbing him in the back?"

"Huh?" Vince said. "What are you talking about?"

"Staples. I saw pictures, Vince. You can't deny it; you

met with Staples this morning."

"Staples? Mac, I don't know what you're . . ." Vince started but then stopped. His eyes glazed over with the sudden realization that he'd been caught. When he spoke again, his voice was weaker, as if he could barely get the words out. "Staples. I should have known."

"Yeah, you *should* have known I'd find out! How could I not? We're supposed to be partners," I said. "Best friends."

"We are partners, Mac. Business partners and friends who spy on each other, apparently. So I guess this means you had Tyrell follow me, then? *Me?*" Vince jabbed his finger against his chest.

He had no right to be the angry one. A fact that was only pissing me off more than I already was.

"Yeah, well, it wasn't such a bad move after all, was it?" I said. "Now where is my money?" I walked over to his closet and started to open it.

Vince pushed me out of the way, and I stumbled, catching myself on his dresser and almost knocking it over. "I told you, I gave it to my mom," he said. "Why do you have to be so greedy all the time? You already have *everything*! Sometimes things are more important than your Funds. We didn't start this business to get rich, remember—it was to help kids."

"Me, greedy? Me? You're the one who took it all! You

stole six thousand dollars and you're calling me greedy? 'Gave it to your mom,' pfft. You're lying about that. You lied about that whole thing, didn't you? I bet your mom didn't even lose her job, did she? I bet you're all just rolling in the cash laughing at me now, aren't you?"

Vince opened his mouth and shook his head. It looked like he was trying to say something, but he just made a small croaking noise.

"Are you happy now?" I asked.

Vince shook his head.

We looked at each other for a moment. "Now, where is it?" I threw open his dresser drawer, fighting tears. "I can't believe you'd throw away the Cubs game just like that. Or did you ever really even like the Cubs? Are you just a phony, like all the others? You pretend to be poor and you pretend to like the Cubs, and all for what? You stab your best friend in the back while hiding behind jokes. You're not even that funny. But you are a coward. And a good liar, I'll give you that."

"Get out," Vince said. He said it quietly and calmly but in a way that I'd never heard Vince talk before. His voice was tight like a wild dog on a short leash. "Get out, right now," he repeated.

"Not without my money," I said.

"Get out or I'll make you," he said, and shoved me in the chest so hard that I crashed into his bedroom wall and made the whole trailer wobble slightly. His face was blank as if emotion had never really existed on it at all. And it probably hadn't. No one with real feelings, with an actual heart, could do what he had done to me.

I realized that all the time I'd been there in his room that afternoon, he'd barely even made an attempt to deny any of my accusations. He really had betrayed me. I felt tears burn at my eyes, but not from my sore head where it had slammed into his wall. That barely hurt at all compared to what else I was feeling. In fact, the lump on my head felt like a day at the carnival complete with cotton candy and funnel cakes just then.

I got up and left, making sure to nudge Vince extra hard with my shoulder on my way out. His mom gave me a concerned look as I walked past her in the kitchen. I heard her start to ask me something, but it was too late. I was already out the door and on my bike before she got past the second word.

The next morning I revealed the news to Joe, Fred, and the bullies. I told them that Vince was the rat. That he had stolen the Emergency and Game Funds. Which meant I was out of money and officially closing up my business.

"I'm sorry I can't pay you what I owe," I said to them solemnly and sincerely. "I've got nothing left."

They reacted surprisingly well. Especially Great White.

They said stuff like, "It's okay, Mac," and "I'm sorry it went down like this."

"Yeah, Mac, this all really stinks. Are you going to be okay?" Joe asked.

"Yeah, I'll be fine. Now, you guys go on and do whatever you got to do. I'm going to stay here awhile and try to get some of my stuff cleaned up," I said.

They all said good-bye and left. Except for Fred.

"Is it okay if I stay, Mac?" he asked.

"Yeah, sure. Whatever you want," I said.

"Thanks. Mac?"

"Yeah," I said, looking down at his face.

His eyes were brimming with tears that should have been mirroring my own, but ever since yesterday I hadn't cried a drop. I'd have thought finding out that my best friend betrayed me in the worst way imaginable would have made me cry like a girl on Valentine's Day, but it was as if I was too broken inside to cry anymore. I just felt nothing. Even thinking of the Cubs making the World Series for the first time in almost seventy years felt meaningless, like a cracked, dead leaf lying on the pavement.

"I'm real sorry about all this. It's all my fault." Fred sobbed.

I assured him that it had been bound to happen sooner or later, with Staples moving in on my school. I apologized to him for failing to protect him and take down Staples like I'd said I was going to. Eventually he stopped crying. I told Fred he was welcome to hang out here for the next few days if he still wanted to. I went into my office and paged through my Books. I wasn't looking for anything in particular. I was mostly just thinking about the good old days when my best friend wasn't also an evil heartless jerk intent on destroying my life.

Chapter 22

That night I decided to go to the junior high football game. I kind of just wanted a break from everything that had happened lately. But I also had some business to take care of. It wasn't pleasant business, but it was perhaps the only way I could salvage the wreck my life had become.

The junior high football games were usually pretty fun. Tons of kids went, and we always sat up in the north corner of the stands away from the parents. Vince and I normally went to every game of the season together. This was actually the first game I'd ever gone to without him. Vince not being there would have felt worse if I didn't ever want to see his lying rat face again.

I wandered the top of the cement bleachers alone.

There was a concession stand and a booth where the radio guys sat and did commentary for the local sports station. Our town was really into sports, so even the junior high games got to be on the radio.

I found a seat near where the parents always sat, away from all the other kids. I just wanted to watch the game and think. As I watched, I began to notice something: Our star running back was playing like garbage. The offensive line would open these huge holes for him to run through, but instead he would try to cut it outside every time, and there was always a linebacker or defensive back just waiting for him. He never seemed to know where to go. It might have seemed odd to a normal spectator. But by this time I knew better.

By halftime he had ten yards on fifteen carries. I saw the coach screaming at him on the sidelines. At the start of the second half the running back was on the bench. The backup running back was in. But that didn't help much, because he was really supposed to be the third-string running back. He was playing only because the usual backup running back had gotten kicked off the team for mouthing off to the coach.

I was clearly watching the handiwork of Staples. He must have paid the starting running back to play poorly on purpose. By the fourth quarter we were down by twenty-six points. A loss was inevitable. Staples must have made a load of money—the team we played that night was terrible and everybody had thought for sure that we'd win. All the fans were pretty disappointed. Plus, losing this game meant that we had to win next week if we still wanted to make the play-offs. The junior high football team had made it to the play-offs every season for over fifty years. People would be crushed if they didn't make it this year, especially the old-timers who used to play themselves. This year's team would be known as the biggest losers in school history—because they literally would be.

Near the end of the game I made my way over to the seats in front of the concession stand where the seventh and eighth graders usually sat. I had work to do now. I had avoided it all night, but it had to be done to keep anybody else from getting hurt. I looked at all of the faces until I saw Justin and Mitch. They were sitting right in the middle of a group of older girls. I cursed the odds. I always get a little nervous around older girls for some dumb reason. But it didn't matter; I had something important to take care of, so I had no time to worry about girls.

I found an open seat just in front of Justin and went over and sat down. I felt people watching me. They were probably wondering where Vince was because we were always together.

After a moment I heard Justin's voice. "What do *you* want?"

"I need to talk to you," I said, turning around to face him.

"*I need to talk to you,*" he mocked me with a high-pitched and nasal voice. Everybody laughed. I didn't think he did a very good job, I didn't sound anything like that, but I just decided to stay quiet about his horrible impression. I just looked at him. I could tell it was making him uneasy.

"So? What is it then, dork?" he sneered. I heard a few giggles.

"I need to talk to Staples," I said.

"Hey, anything you need to say to him, you can say to me, okay?"

"Okay. I want to accept his offer for me to come work for him," I said. "I want to make a truce, I guess, in exchange for him letting Fred off the hook."

It was one of the hardest things I'd ever had to say. Normally I'm not the type of kid to give up, but I still know when I'm beat. And dragging this out to the end was only going to bring Joe and Fred and the bullies more trouble than they needed. If I surrendered now, maybe I could avoid all the insult and injury headed my way. I had to keep telling myself that I wasn't quitting. There are times when making a bargain just makes more sense than fighting to the end. This was one of those times.

Justin's jaw dropped. I bet he hadn't even known that

Staples had made me that offer. Mitch whispered something in Justin's ear. Justin nodded and finally closed his mouth.

"How do I know this isn't some kind of trick?" he asked uneasily.

"You don't."

The kids around us all got quiet. They were all watching us now.

"Look, he made me the offer," I said. "If you want to go to him and say you turned me away because you didn't believe me and then have to deal with how mad he's going to be, go right ahead."

He thought about it for a moment. I could see him struggling to decide what to do. He'd never seemed all that smart to me. Now I could see why Staples wanted me to work for him. His current employees at my school were idiots. Except for one, of course.

"Okay, sure, I'll tell him," Justin finally said.

"Tell him to meet me in my office on Monday after school at three thirty. I'll make sure that the East Wing entrance is left unlocked for him."

I left Justin there gaping and walked back up the steps to the top of the bleachers. If I was going to surrender, then I at least wanted it to be on my turf.

Once the game ended, I saw the players heading toward the shower house. It was this small building off to the side of the field that had showers and locker rooms in it for the players. Parents and friends would always group around there and wait for the team. I saw Robert, the kid I'd helped right before Fred on that fateful Monday when everything changed forever, taking off his helmet. Robert, the last regular, simple customer in the history of my business. Robert, who paid with a small favor to help get him and a date into an R-rated movie because his dad's a cop and . . .

His dad's a cop.

And he still owed me a favor.

It wasn't much, but I supposed there was still time for one last desperation play. A Hail Mary. They rarely ever worked, I knew that, but at the same time, people like Doug Flutie would swear otherwise.

I jogged down to the shower house and waited around until Robert came out. He went straight to his parents and this older girl. I assumed it was his new girlfriend because she rubbed his arm and gave him a hug. His dad patted him on the shoulder, consoling him over the loss.

I positioned myself behind his parents so that I knew he'd see me. After a few minutes I saw him say something to them and jog over to me. His parents went to get their car.

"Hey, Mac, what's up?" he said.

"Hi, Robert. Sorry about the game."

"Yeah, I don't know what happened out there. We were opening the holes; he just wasn't hitting them. . . ."

"Even the star running back has bad games, right?" I said.

Robert shrugged.

"Your dad is a cop, right?" I asked.

"Yeah, why?" Robert asked with raised eyebrows.

"I may need your help, and his," I said.

He nodded. "Hey, I owe you."

"I need to get someone's name and address and criminal record. Do you think you might be able to get that from your dad somehow?" I asked.

He sighed and then said, "Yeah, I think so. He's pretty careful about not using cop stuff for anything but business, but I think I can swing it."

"Good. Okay, I'm looking for someone who goes by the alias Staples. If any hits come up for an address in the Creek, then you'll know you got the right guy."

I remembered from that first meeting with Staples in my kitchen that he has a tattoo that says "The Creek." A lot of kids who live there are actually proud of it and they're always drawing those words all over their notebooks and lockers and stuff. They wear "The Creek" like some sort of badge of honor. So I had a pretty good hunch that that's where I'd find Staples's headquarters.

"Do you mean *the* Staples?" Robert asked. "I

thought he didn't exist."

"Yeah, well, he does. I need his real name, address, criminal record, and anything else you can dig up as soon as possible. Tonight, if you can." I gave him a piece of paper with my phone number on it.

"All right, Mac. I'll try. I'll call you when I know more."

"Thanks a lot, Robert, really."

"No problem, Mac."

I walked back up the hill toward my parents' waiting car. I wished my plan felt more like a suicide squeeze than a Hail Mary. With the suicide squeeze you have the upper hand. The other side is on defense and always has to be wary of that guy on third base. The play is a thing of precision, timing, grace, beauty. It's smooth and fast and sneaks up on the opponent like a dagger to the kidney. But my newest idea was much more like a Hail Mary: desperate, fleeting, clumsy, and chaotic. No thought, no timing, no synchronization; basically just chuck it up in the air and hope for the best. It's more likely to lead to an interception than anything helpful. But it was all I had left.

Robert called me late that night.

"Tell me something good, Big Guy," I said as I answered.

"I've got it, Mac. I've got it all."

"Seriously?"

"Hey, when I owe somebody something, I like to deliver. Anyways, Staples's real name is Barry Larsen and he lives at 1808 Academy Road South. At the Creek, just like you said. His rap sheet is a mile long. He's been arrested for vandalism, burglary, racketeering, contributing to the delinquency of a minor, disturbing the peace; I could list them forever. He's on probation and he's got like two years of suspended sentences. Basically, if the cops catch wind that he's up to something, he's going away for a long time."

The name Barry Larsen seemed familiar to me much in the same way that Staples himself had when I first saw him, but I still couldn't quite figure out why. I was pretty sure I didn't know anyone by that name. But it didn't really matter—this was a huge discovery for me regardless of whether I recognized the name or not.

"Great work, Robert. I can't begin to thank you enough," I said.

"Mac, I already told you that I owed you, remember?" Robert said. "Don't worry about it. Plus, you're a good guy. You deserve it."

We hung up and I celebrated just a little bit. It felt empty, though, without Vince. Also, to be fair, what I had in mind was still a long shot. And it was still incredibly dangerous. Like walking into the girls' bathroom alone and unarmed.

Chapter 23

I got up early on Saturday. Earlier than I can remember getting up in a long time on a weekend. I had a lot to do, not unlike most weekends, but on most weekends I had a business partner to help me.

I rode my bike to Tyrell's house. He didn't live far from me, but I had only been to his place a few times and I almost rode right past it. His house was surrounded by several evergreen trees and a patch of bushes, and it had been painted to match the trees and bushes around it. You seriously almost had to do a double take even to see the house when riding past on a bike.

I walked up the sidewalk to where I thought there'd be a front door, but there wasn't one. It was just solid wood siding like the rest of the front of the house. I would have laughed if I still had a reason left to laugh ever again.

I headed slowly around toward the back of the house, and that's when a chunk of tree almost crashed down on top of me. I let out a yell and then composed myself when I realized I was still in one piece. But I have to admit I almost passed out when the chunk of tree talked to me.

"What's up, Mac?" it said.

"Uh . . ." was all I managed to say back.

The large tree branch stood up, and I finally saw the two eyes and mouth behind all of the face paint and fake foliage. I shook my head and this time, and in spite of everything that had happened, I laughed.

"You're nuts," I said.

Tyrell just shrugged. "Just testing some things out," he said. "What do you need?"

"Well, I was wondering if you'd be willing to accept another assignment from me."

He nodded but said nothing.

"Unfortunately . . ." I started, but had to stop. I could have sworn the bush behind Tyrell had just moved a few feet. I stared at it a moment longer but it was still. "Anyways, like I was saying, I can't pay you right now. My money has been stolen. I will try to pay you eventually, but right now—"

"Mac," Tyrell said with his hands up. "It's all right; you don't have to explain anything to me. I know you're good for it. Besides, I like the challenges you present. They are like no other."

"Thanks, Tyrell. You're a pal, you know that?"

"I am what I want to be. Nothing more, nothing less."

I smirked at this, while once again trying to ignore the fact that the bush seemed to be several feet closer than it had been just a few moments before.

"Anyways, I'd like for you to case a joint for me. Stake it out all day today and call me as soon as the coast is clear. And bring some of your tools. Hopefully we'll be doing a little B and E as well, if you know what I mean."

Tyrell grinned. "I got just the stuff. What's the address?"

"It's . . ." I stopped again since this time the bush had *definitely* moved. Plus, there seemed to be a head-shaped bulge of leaves sticking out from the top of it. "What the . . ."

Tyrell turned around, glanced at the bush, and chuckled. "Oh, that. Don't worry about that—that's just my mom. She's still got some things to learn about *opportunities of undetected motion*, a basic principle of Incognito Methodology."

I shook my head and laughed again. After giving Tyrell Staples's address, I started back toward my bike, making a mental note to see if Tyrell was in the market for a new best friend, being that I needed one myself.

Before I got to my bike, I tripped on a mound in the grass and nearly fell.

"Ow!" the grass said. "Watch where you're going."

I turned around to see a head pop up from the ground. It was covered in grass, but it was clearly human. And clearly annoyed with me. I could now see a whole person was lying on the grass wearing some kind of full body grass suit.

"Sorry, that's just my sister," Tyrell called out from the tree he was once again perched in.

I shook my head and threw a quick wave at the branch that I thought was Tyrell. I got back on my bike and pedaled for home, perhaps a little faster than I had on the way there. Sure, they're a funny family, and I have to give them credit for making me laugh at the darkest point in my whole life. But they still gave me the creeps a little bit.

Tyrell called me later that afternoon.

"Mac, he's gone. PJ and a few girls showed up and they all left together in one car with a few coolers. I don't think they'll be back for a while."

"Nice work," I said. "Wait there. I'll be down as soon as I can."

Staples's house wasn't too far from Vince's, but I took an alternate route to make sure I stayed well clear of that liar's pit of deception. I never wanted to see his trailer again. It took me about twenty minutes to get to Staples's address.

The house at his address wasn't really much of a house at all. It was small and white with old, chipped paint. Half of the porch was partially caved in. The red sports car that had almost killed me sat in the driveway, soaking up the sun like it was trying to get a nice tan.

It was a little nerve-racking to be in this neighborhood by myself. I looked around for Tyrell and didn't see any sign of him. I walked my bike to the trash cans near the curb and that's when a head poked up from the trash.

"Hey, Mac," Tyrell said.

I nodded at him, this time not really all that surprised he had been staking out the place disguised as garbage. He climbed out of the garbage can and took off a plastic trash bag he'd been wearing. Underneath he wore black pants and a dark blue shirt and those rubber purple gloves I've seen doctors and nurses sometimes wearing at hospitals. He handed me a pair and I put them on without asking.

We sat behind the garbage cans for a few minutes and just watched the place. Everything was still. I had a few basic questions I wanted answers to, but I wasn't really there for anything specific. Basically, I was looking for anything, anything at all that might help me get out of this mess.

We approached the gate to the side of the house, Tyrell in the lead. He moved so quickly and quietly that I could have sworn his feet were floating just above the grass. The gate was solid wood and rose just higher than my head. I grabbed the top and pulled myself up just high enough to see into the backyard.

The grass was yellow, long, and weedy. There was a shed in the back corner. Next to that was a small doghouse with a sleeping pit bull inside of it. That would not exactly be helpful when trying to check out the place, but we'd deal with that later. Tyrell had also pulled himself up, and I gave him a look as he dropped beside me.

He shook his head and whispered, "Don't worry. The dog won't be a problem."

I wasn't sure how he could be so confident, but I trusted that he knew what he was doing.

The first thing I needed to know was whether Staples had parents that we had to worry about. Whether the house was truly empty right now or not. I tapped Tyrell and motioned for him to follow me toward the porch.

We moved around to the front of the house and crept up the steps. They creaked under our feet. Tyrell stayed back to watch the street while I approached the front door. I heard Staples's dog start barking in the backyard.

Their mailbox hung next to the front door. It was the kind that's just like a huge 3-D metal envelope stuck to the house. I lifted the flap and flinched a little when it creaked loudly.

The mailbox had a magazine and a few letters in it. One was an energy bill—I could tell because the envelope had the local energy company's logo on it. There was a FINAL NOTICE stamp on the front. I looked through the clear plastic on the envelope; it was addressed to Jonah Larsen. I wasn't sure what to make of that quite yet. The other letters were also addressed to Jonah Larsen. One of them was from a place called Ahmed Collections. Another was from the IRS, which was a pretty evil tax organization, based on what I'd gathered from movies and TV shows.

Then I looked at the magazine, which was addressed to Barry Larsen. It was called *Ink and Ammo*. On the cover it had a ridiculous picture of this shirtless guy with rippling muscles and tons of tattoos shooting a gigantic machine gun. The caption read, "Inside: 10 Secrets to Showing Off Your Guns."

I figured that Jonah was either Staples's dad or older brother. I put the mail back into the metal box and walked over to a dirty window a few feet away. It was overcast that day but still bright, and the light kept me from seeing inside, so I cupped my hands around my eyes and pressed my face up against the dirty glass. The inside was a disaster. There were dirty clothes and empty pizza boxes everywhere. Near a ratty orange couch, there was even a pile of dog poop that looked like it had been there since the 1880s. But it was what was on the couch that shocked me most.

It was an old guy. He was wearing only gray sweat-pants and a single black sock. And he was lying on his back with one leg dangling over the back of the couch. His face was sweaty and unshaven and he was clearly sleeping, possibly in a deep coma. It was a pretty gross sight. There were empty cans scattered all across the guy's living room. Some of them were crushed flat, but I doubted that was because they were going to get recycled.

It was the same guy who Vince and I had seen out at the lake cabin. Staples's dad, I was sure of it. So that red car had been the same car after all, and that lady must have been Staples's dad's girlfriend or something like that. I remembered then what she had said about his son paying his bills. So that's what Staples did with all the money he made after all.

It explained a lot. Staples was essentially doing the same thing Vince *claimed* to be doing for his mom.

Maybe that's why they had apparently bonded over stealing my money. They were both helping out their own poor families. It almost made me sympathize with what they'd done to me, but then I quickly squashed that thought. Even if they were doing this to help their families, there were better ways to go about it. Ways that didn't involve lying, cheating, backstabbing, betrayal, beatings, intimidation, and theft.

The scene on the couch was a pretty gross and sad sight, but at least from the look of it, we probably would not have to worry about the guy waking up and catching us snooping around. Or if he did, he'd never be able to catch us if we ran. I went back to where Tyrell was crouched near the front steps and filled him in on what I'd seen.

"Let's go," he said, and nodded his head toward the gate to the backyard.

Staples's pit bull was still barking, and once we got there, I peeked over the fence. He was just a few feet away from the fence gate, held back by a chain attached to the doghouse. Tyrell must have seen the look on my face because he just grinned and then climbed over the gate to the other side.

I shrugged to no one in particular and then climbed over myself. The dog was only a few feet away from us and was frothing at the mouth the way rabid animals do in cartoons. The chain holding him at bay started to strain under his pull.

"What now?" I asked.

Tyrell reached into his messenger bag and pulled out a hunk of tinfoil. He unwrapped it and revealed a pretty sizable steak. The oldest trick in the book, sure, but did it work in real life?

Then Tyrell took off running to my left. It wasn't really what I was expecting him to do, and I froze, unable to take my eyes off the pit bull snapping at his heels. Tyrell stayed just ahead of the dog, dangling the steak behind him. He wove around a tree and then back around another just a few feet away. The dog followed, getting so close that he actually was able to clip one of Tyrell's shoes in his jaws and tear it right off his foot.

But then the chain, which was now woven and wrapped tightly around two trees, pulled tight and the dog yelped and jerked back. He was stuck well out of range of me now, and there was a clear path to the shed. The dog continued to bark at Tyrell, who taunted him with the steak as he put his shoe back on.

Then Tyrell tossed the steak at the dog, who ignored it at first and just kept snarling. But then eventually the dog lost interest in us and lay down with the steak clutched between his two paws. Tyrell walked back over to where I was standing and grinned at me.

"Nice trick," I said. "How did you know you'd need that? Or do you always walk around with a two-pound steak in your bag?"

Tyrell didn't answer but just motioned for me to follow him.

We approached the shed. It was padlocked shut. Tyrell dug into his bag and then removed a chunk of metal kind of shaped like a gun. But instead of a barrel or muzzle it just had these two long, thin rods. He stuck the rods into the lock along with another L-shaped piece of metal he held in his other hand. He pulled the "trigger" of the gun while turning the other metal rod like a key. The padlock clicked open, just like that.

And then we were inside. It was warm, but Tyrell switched on a nearby electric fan. He also clicked on a naked lightbulb dangling from the ceiling of the moderately sized shed. If it was empty, it would have been just about the right size to store a Jet Ski or a few motorcycles and not much else. But it wasn't empty. Inside were a large desk, a few chairs, and a few old file cabinets.

Staples's office.

It looked pretty similar to my own. Which surprised me, though I wasn't really sure why. It's not like I expected his office to be made of bones and jagged rocks and have miniature volcanoes inside it shooting out fireballs. I think the surprise was that someone so mean and supposedly evil could also be so organized.

We started digging. On his desk were a few notebooks containing lists of kids who owed him money. As much as I was curious to see who was in there, that wasn't something that could help me much at that moment. There were also a lot of old sports newspapers and magazines lying around.

Staples had a ridiculous bobblehead collection lining some shelves behind his desk. They were mostly baseball players. He practically had the whole Yankees lineup and half the Hall of Fame. I was a little jealous of the collection, to be honest. And I was surprised that such a psycho could appreciate the finer things in life, such as baseball.

There was some other stuff scattered about that didn't look related to his business, like a few baseball gloves and an old TV with an ancient-looking, gray video game system I didn't recognize hooked up to it. On his desk was a picture of a really little girl and Staples standing next to the same shed we were in. The picture was old—Staples looked maybe close to my age in it— but it was definitely him. Only in the picture, the lawn around the shed was green and freshly cut and the shed was newly painted and Staples actually looked nice. And happy. I could only guess that the girl in the picture might be a little sister. I wondered where she was now.

I certainly hoped she didn't still live there. That house was no place for anybody to live in, let alone a little girl. The photo was just another item that left me suddenly feeling a little uncertain as to just who Staples really is, and what his intentions were.

That's when it all finally clicked. I suddenly knew why he'd looked so familiar to me. Barry Larsen was an older kid who used to live in our trailer park. We used to play football with him. We had done so on the very day I'd met Vince for the first time. Staples had actually invited me to play football with him when we were kids. In fact, I even caught a pass from him that day, and I remember he said, "Hey, nice catch, kid." I'd almost passed out, I was so proud that an older kid complimented me. Barry Larsen had never seemed like such a bad guy. I marveled at the discovery, but pressed on with the search.

Tyrell moved on to the file cabinets, and I started rummaging through his desk. If you want the truth, I honestly expected to find my stolen Funds right then and there that day. Where else would he have them hidden? But we didn't find my money. We didn't find *any* money, actually. But just because we didn't find my money doesn't mean we didn't find anything useful. In fact, we found plenty. What we saw in Staples's shed that day changed everything.

Chapter 24

Monday passed quickly. Too quickly. For once I wanted the hours in class to drag, to last forever. And for once, class time flew by. Funny how that works, isn't it?

For the most part Fred and I didn't talk during any of the recess or lunch breaks. He played DS while I sat in my office, going over my final Books, trying to predict whether or not Staples would actually show up after school. Right at the end of afternoon recess, I called Fred into my office.

"Yeah?" he asked as he stepped into the fourth stall from the high window.

"Fred, do you think you could meet me here after school today?" I asked.

"Sure, I guess. My mom said she'd be home late today anyways."

"Thanks. Just meet me here at three twenty-five. The door will be open."

"Okay," he said, standing up. "I guess I'll see you then." He opened the stall's door.

"And Fred, one last thing," I said, prompting him to stop before leaving the stall. "Don't be late."

"Okay," he said.

The bell rang a short time later. I had just a few hours left until my meeting with Staples. Maybe only had a few hours left to live, depending on how it would all go down.

After class I packed my stuff into my backpack and trudged across the school to my office. My stomach ached like it knew something I didn't, which was a strange feeling for me. I wasn't used to being so nervous and jittery all the time. Just a few weeks ago I had been in total control of this school. Or I thought I had been. Now I had been reduced to nothing but some friendless, penniless kid with a key to an abandoned bathroom in the boonies of the school's East Wing.

The halls were crowded that day, but the kids didn't shout greetings like they normally did. I had been pretty popular around here simply because of what I could do for people. But lately kids seemed to care less. I think they knew my business was all but finished. Too many kids had witnessed my surrender plea to Justin Friday night at the football game, and my office had hardly been open at all in the past two weeks.

I got to the East Wing entrance and waited there for the janitor. He locked the door every day at 3:20. Only two of the school's eight entrances remained unlocked after 3:30. And those only stayed open until four o'clock.

"Hey, Mac, how are you?" he said as he reached for his keys.

"I'm okay. Say, a friend is coming to visit me, so do you think you could leave this one open until 4:00 today?" I asked.

"Sure, no problem," he said, and walked back down the hallway. He whistled some catchy tune that I recognized from somewhere.

Just like that. No questions asked. You don't ask questions that don't need to be answered. That's rule number one when dealing with a business like mine. And the janitor seemed to understand that. He was by far the coolest adult I had ever met. Kids in most schools make fun of their janitors because it's usually some creepy guy with gross hair, a funny smell, and a collection of bent spoons in his work closet. But our janitor is downright awesome.

I went inside the bathroom and sat in my office. Fred

entered a few moments later. I heard him sit in one of the chairs across from the sink. It was three minutes until three thirty. I wasn't sure if Staples would show. And if he did, could I go through with it?

The first question was answered just a minute later, when the door to the bathroom swung open. I heard heavy footsteps scuff across the dirty tile floor. Then I heard Fred's voice.

"Staples? What are you doing here?"

Fred didn't sound all that shocked to see Staples, though. You'd have thought he would sound terrified. But he didn't. There was a silence and then Fred spoke again.

"Uh, Mac, Staples is here! Why is Staples here?"

I got up and stepped out of my office. Fred was still seated in his plastic chair and Staples stood by the sink a few feet away. They were both looking at me.

"Oh, Fred, I think you know why Staples is here," I said.

Fred shook his head, "I don't. I don't know what—"

But Staples cut him off. "So I heard you finally want to accept my offer? Having problems with your business, are you?"

I looked at Staples with a blank face. I didn't really feel all that afraid of him anymore. Because this time, for once, I actually did have the drop on him. This time

I had the element of surprise.

"I guess you could say that," I said, trying to sound calm, bored. "But I most definitely do *not* want to accept your offer."

His eyes narrowed. "Then why am I here? I don't like being jerked around, Christian."

"Yeah, well, I don't like being jerked around either, *Barry*."

He shook his head and took a step back. He looked so shocked that I knew his real name that I thought he might have a heart attack right there in my office.

"How? How do you know my name?" he demanded.

"All in due time," I said. "First, I have an offer to make you. Well, it's more of a demand than an offer. One: I want you out of my school forever. I don't want to hear about any of my classmates placing a bet with one of your bookies again. Two: I don't ever want to see you or any of your high school cronies near my friends ever again."

Staples laughed. He had gone from scowling and confused to laughing in just a second's time.

"So . . . so . . . ." He tried to talk but was too busy laughing.

I waited while he calmed down.

Eventually he composed himself enough to say, "So what exactly are you going to do if I refuse your offer?" When he said the word "offer," he made bunny ears with two fingers from each of his hands and then curled his fingertips downward.

"Well, right now, as we speak, a few friends of mine are currently raiding the shed in your backyard. They're going to kidnap your dog, search the place, and take any money or information that they find. They're going to call me in the next few minutes to confirm all of this, and if I don't answer, they'll know something is wrong, and they'll take your dog out to a field and leave him there, call the cops and give them all the stuff they found, and keep all of your cash. Which, to answer your question, is also basically what will happen if you refuse our offer." I made the same bunny-ears-curl-downward gesture, then pulled my phone from my pocket so Staples could see it.

"I don't believe you," he said, but he was no longer smiling.

"No? Your address is 1808 Academy Road South. Your dog is a pit bull with a pink camouflage collar. Your office is in a shed in your backyard, and you have a pretty remarkable bobblehead doll collection. My friends will use a bolt cutter to break into your shack. They'll use sleeping pills to disarm your dog. Oh, and they better find my Emergency and Game Funds, too, because I want those back."

Staples shook his head. He looked a little shocked and maybe a little scared, but also very, very angry. He rubbed his left eye and then balled his hand into a fist. His knuckles turned white as snow.

"But I don't have your stupid little Funds. How could I have stolen them? I don't even know where they are," he snarled.

"I know, but your snitch does." I turned to Fred. His eyes went wide.

I continued. "Fred knew where I hid my Funds and he told you where they were. Then breaking into my room Thursday afternoon probably wasn't all that hard, was it, Barry? Considering that you found my window open? I still can't believe that Fred has been working for you all this time." I looked down at him in the chair.

Fred looked away quickly.

"I know it was you, Fred. You broke my heart."

He looked at his feet. I could tell he was ashamed of himself. He shook his head and whined, "He made me do it, Mac!"

"Whatever, Fred. It doesn't matter now." I looked back at Staples. "You see, I found a Nintendo DS inside your desk, Staples, when I broke into your shed on Saturday. It struck me as odd that you would be into the DS, being that most of its games are for little kids. So I powered it up and found something pretty shocking: messages from Fred in the in-box. All the time I'd thought Fred had been playing games on his DS, he was really taking notes with the stylus and sending them to you.

"I also found a few records in the file cabinets detailing who is still on your payroll, and sure enough Fred is listed. And Vince isn't. Up to that point I really had thought that Vince was the snitch and had stolen the Funds. I really had believed that Fred was innocent and had been telling the truth about everything and that I was ruined. It had all added up. It had all made such perfect sense. And that's because that's what you had wanted me to think all along, isn't it, Staples? You're clever, I have to admit that. You staged everything to make me think Vince stole the Funds and was the snitch."

Staples just stared at me and didn't say anything.

Sure, I was happy when I found out I was wrong, that my best friend hadn't stabbed me in the back. But the news had also hit me like a three-ton semitruck going one hundred miles per hour. Because it meant I had questioned my best friend's loyalty in the worst way imaginable. And thinking back to everything I'd said to him, no wonder he was so angry he could barely even talk or deny my accusations. I'd acted like a true jerk not to trust him or even give him the chance to explain.

Which made it extra hard to go visit him on Sunday morning to try and apologize. When I got to his trailer and his mom answered the door, the first things I saw on her face were relief and then a smile.

"Christian, I'm so glad you're here," she said. "I don't know what happened between you guys on Thursday, and it's none of my business, but he's barely even left his room since then. He hasn't changed, showered, anything. I can barely even get him to eat."

I hadn't thought I could feel much worse up to that point but I had been wrong. I wanted to compost myself and let some crazy lady use me as fertilizer for her tomato plants. I wanted to cover myself in honey and then get lowered slowly into a huge vat of fire ants. I wanted to strip the skin off my arms with a cheese grater and then take a lemon juice bath. I wanted to poke a sleeping lion in the ribs with a short stick. I wanted . . . Okay, you probably get the idea.

"Well, I'll see what I can do," I said, walking past Vince's mom.

I went to his room and saw that the sign I'd given him for his birthday was no longer hanging on his door. Really, would there ever be an end to just how low I could feel?

I knocked. Nothing.

I knocked again. Again, nothing.

I slowly opened the door and poked my head inside. What I saw, I will never forget, though I wish I could. Vince was lying on his bed wearing the same clothes he'd been wearing on Thursday when we had our fight. His face was the color of cigarette smoke or one of George

Romero's zombies. His eyes were vacant and he lay motionless, and for just a second I thought I *was* looking at an actual zombie. Which was fine, because you can add getting my brains eaten to the list of things I deserved right then.

But then he saw me and spoke.

"What are you doing here?" he said so quietly it was nearly a whisper. "Get out. Don't ever come back."

"I know. I am the worst friend you could have. I should have at least talked to you before jumping to conclusions. All I want is fifteen minutes to try and make things better. After that I'll leave, I'll give you my three Ryne Sandberg rookie cards, I'll do whatever you want. I'll even finally try eating waffles with hand lotion for syrup like your grandma sometimes tries to feed us."

He glanced at me and looked away. But he did sit up and I thought that a little color might have returned to his face. He nodded at me to continue. Like a true friend would.

"First, Vince, I'm sorry I believed that you could have done that to me. It was ridiculous of me to think that, and you have a right to be mad. But just at least try to imagine how it looked from my standpoint. Please. Before this you'd never lied to me before. And then within days of each other I find out that you lied to me about your grandma's birthday, you've been stealing money from our business, and you accepted a payment from Staples. Then my Funds go missing on the one day you happen to miss school for the first time in years?"

"Our Funds."

"What?"

"You said 'my Funds,' but they were *our* Funds," Vince said, still not looking at me.

"Yeah," I said. "They were."

"You're right. I can see how that probably looked bad," Vince said. "But still . . ."

"I know, Vince. I should have trusted you above all else. That's why our business succeeded in the first place. I remembered that when I was thinking about how it was your idea for me to first hire Tyrell back during the Graffiti Ninja debacle. I remembered that it was all you who got this business started in the first place. It was your idea from the start because you recognized what we could do together even as kindergartners. And I should have remembered those things when it mattered most, but I didn't. And I can't really forgive myself for that.

"This whole thing had me feeling paranoid. I just didn't trust anybody anymore, not even myself. And I guess sometimes I lost sight of the fact that this business has always been about you and me, not the money at all. It has never mattered how much money we made, not even for a Cubs World Series game. But I'm not going to make those mistakes again. You're probably the funniest, most trustworthy kid I've ever met. I can't believe I ignored that fact even for a day, or an hour, or a second."

Vince sighed. "I'm sorry, too. This whole thing wasn't all your fault. I mean, I *stole* money from you. That's about as honest as telling a chimp that having thumbs on your feet makes up for having to wear a diaper."

I let out a laugh in spite of the mood. "Your grandma?"

"No," Vince said, shaking his head slowly. "My mom."

"Oh," I said, and stopped smiling. I remembered then that he had said she'd been acting crazy since losing her job. I guess I kind of knew how she felt because I'd kind of lost my job recently, too.

"So what I'm saying is I forgive you if you forgive me for stealing money and lying to you," Vince said.

"Well, before you go getting all sappy on me, I need to know one thing," I said. "What was the deal with taking money from Staples?"

Vince actually chuckled. "That's the thing, Mac. I had no idea that Barry Larsen was Staples. It still just blows me away. I grew up with that kid. He used to live just seven trailers down from me!"

"I know, it shocked me when I found out, too," I said. "I remember playing football with him once or twice."

·271·

"Deep down I think I kind of knew something was up when he stopped by that morning because I hadn't talked to Barry in a while, but I was so desperate for money, I think I just switched off my common sense there for a second."

"But why did he give it to you? Why did you miss school that day?"

"Barry's been trying to get me to sell my bike to him for years," Vince said. "This time he offered me three hundred and fifty bucks for it and I just couldn't resist. I mean, that pays our electric bill for like three months. He paid me half and then said that he'd be by later that day sometime before three to pick it up and pay the other half. So I faked sick and stayed home. I know that whole scenario is so suspicious and I should have known better, but being in this kind of mess does things to you. I especially should have known better when he never came by to get it. I mean, what kid just forgets to collect the merchandise at that price? I can't believe I was that stupid."

Vince must have been really strapped for cash to be willing to sell his bike. It was his dad's bike when he was a kid, a true vintage. For him to sell it for under a grand, or even sell it at all for any price, meant that things really were pretty bad for his family. It was basically the last part of his dad that Vince had left.

"Okay, deal. I forgive you if you forgive me," I said.

"Cue the music," Vince said as he started wiping at his eyes dramatically.

I laughed. "Whatever."

"I still can't believe you questioned my Cubs fandom. Especially after I'm about to finally beat you," Vince said.

"Bring it on," I said.

"What Hall-of-Fame Cub had the nickname Three Finger?"

That was a tough one. I tried to clear my head, which was difficult considering I still had to deal with the Staples issue. Though, really, now that I had Vince back on my side, I felt like we could take down anybody. I felt like if we were playing on the Cubs together as pitcher and catcher right then, we'd break a hundred-year-plus curse that even guys like Greg Maddux and Mark Grace and Aramis Ramirez and Carlos Zambrano and Ernie Banks hadn't been able to break.

"Mordecai Brown," I finally said.

Vince shook his head in defeat. "Well, then."

I grinned at him. "All right, Vince. We still have to deal with Staples somehow. A lot has happened since I last talked to you."

I proceeded to fill him in on the weekend's events. We called over Joe and the bullies and filled them in as well.

And then it was time to plan. We stayed up well past dark Sunday formulating the master plan for Monday.

So that's everything that had happened since Saturday, and everything that had led me up to this point. What happened next would all depend upon how Staples reacted to my offer. He was either going to accept and we'd all go home, or he would decline and the cops would be called in. Then again, there was always option three: He'd ignore my offer and simply beat me to a bloody pulp.

Chapter 25

Staples stood next to the sink near the fourth stall from the high window and glared at me. I took the silence as a chance to ask something that had been bothering me ever since I'd found out that Fred was the snitch.

"I guess there's still one thing I don't get, though, and that's why. Why would you send in Fred to reveal yourself when you could have just kept operating right under my nose?" I asked.

"You can't figure it out for yourself?" Staples sneered. "I thought you were a genius or something. Well, I'll spell it out, then. Rumor had it that you ran a pretty tight business, that you solved *everybody's* problems. And, well, I knew that eventually all the little wusses around here would go and whine and cry to you about how they had lost all their money, and 'Staples is threatening me,' and blah, blah, blah, and you'd stick your big nose into my business. So I struck first. I knew that if I could take out your lame little business that I'd be home free to do whatever I wanted in this school.

"So I sent Fred in. And I knew that if I gave him a story where he'd need constant protection, you'd keep him close. Close enough to get all the information I'd need to wipe you out. Because that's one thing my dead-beat father actually taught me. He taught me: keep your friends close but your enemies closer. And sure enough, it didn't take long for me to know everything. The money was just a bonus. Once Fred told me about your Emergency Fund, it became all about getting that first. Once Fred told me about your argument with your friend, I saw my chance both to get the money and finish you off in one move. I could have wiped you out in just a few days had I really wanted to."

I saw Fred looking at the floor, appearing more sheepish than ever. Staples laughed. He sounded like a maniac.

"I tried to warn you to just back off, too. I sent you so many warnings. At first I was only trying to make sure that you stayed out of my way, but no, you kept on pushing. You didn't mind your own business and then you forced me to take you out. You're such a stubborn little pest, trying to play gangster like it's some game."

I thought about what he said. It didn't really add up. He had been trying to take me out from the beginning. He had just told me so. He only delayed and sent warnings to keep me off his back long enough to give Fred a chance to steal my money. No, he was trying to turn the tables and make me doubt myself.

"I never wanted to hurt you, Christian; you kept bringing it on yourself."

"No. This was your fault, *Barry*, not mine. I'm not the one with a dirty business. I make my money by providing a service, not by cheating kids. Plus, you *did* want to hurt me. How else can you explain sending Willis and that other kid after me, or trying to kill me with your car? You're jealous, aren't you? That's why you've had it out for me from the beginning. You're jealous that I have a business that works without cheating, that some little kid can run a smoother, more profitable business than you. And you're jealous that I have a dad who's not some drunken deadbeat slob."

Staples shook his head. He seemed at a loss for words. Finally he said, "No, Christian, you're wrong!" His teeth were pressed together and spit flew from his mouth when he talked.

That's when my phone rang. All three of us looked at

it as it sat in my hand.

"Excuse me," I said, and flipped the phone open.

"Hey, Mac! We got it, all of it. It worked perfectly," Vince's voice said. He sounded as excited as I'd ever heard him.

"Good," I said, and smiled at Staples. He did not smile back.

"We got almost all of our money back. It was in a lockbox under the floorboards, right where Tyrell knew to look. And we got documents and business records and all kinds of incriminating stuff, too. How are things there?" Vince said.

"Good. Hang on a minute, Vince," I said.

"What? What?" Staples said. He sounded menacing, but he looked worried.

"They got it," I said. "They got it all. They even found my money under the floorboards."

That's when Staples moved like lightning. He stepped forward and smacked the phone right out of my hand. It smashed into the concrete wall and clattered onto the floor in several pieces. I backed up, but I had nowhere to go.

"What are you doing? They'll call the cops!" I said.

But I wasn't sure if they actually would. We never actually thought it would come to that.

"You really think the cops will care about some kid

taking bets?" Staples said.

"They will when the perp has a list of priors as long as California. I know you're on probation, so one little incident and you're going to prison. You'll have to write me, Barry, and let me know what the slammer is like. I've always been curious about that."

Staples's eyes turned pure red. His hands made fists, and I heard his teeth grind together. He punched a nearby stall door and it dented with a bang. I flinched. Then he punched the mirror and it splintered and a few shards shattered on the tile floor. I looked at his fist as he turned to face me; it wasn't pretty.

"Well, it doesn't look like I have a choice, then, does it?" Staples said with such intense vehemence that it almost made me want to die in fear right there on the spot.

"Your choice is to leave my school forever or go to prison," I said quietly.

"No, no. I don't have a choice. You're a sneaky little liar and you're going to turn me in no matter what I say, aren't you?" he said, taking a few more steps toward me.

I backed up more and realized that I was now cornered. I was back by the high window with nowhere to go.

"No! I wouldn't do that. I keep my word. A deal is a deal."

"Right. Just like you lied to me to get me here, right?" he said.

"No, that was just . . . I mean . . . I swear I'll give you your stuff back, all I want is *my* money that *you* stole," I said, trying to take the offensive.

He laughed and moved within a few feet of me.

"Well, here's the thing: your little friends can do whatever they want with the stuff they stole from my shed. Let them call the cops. All you need to worry about is the fact that *you* will pay for it." He was speaking so harshly that his spit sprinkled my face. "I'm already going to prison, right? So who cares if they add more time for what I'm about to do to you?"

I knew he was done bargaining. Staples had gone off the deep end. I kicked out my foot at his shin, but he was too fast. He stepped away from my kick and I lost my balance. Then he moved with mongooselike speed and grabbed my wrist. His bony fingers dug into my arm.

I yelped in pain and tried to get away, but his grip was like a bear trap.

"Fred, help me!" I yelled.

He just cowered even more in his chair. His feet were up on the seat and his arms were wrapped around his legs. He had basically curled into a little ball like an armadillo under duress.

At that point I realized that I had no choice but to

fight dirty. I grabbed the hand that was holding my wrist and pulled my face to it. He tried to push my head away with his other hand, but it was too late. I didn't really want to do it, but I closed my eyes and bit. Staples yelled in pain and let go of me.

Then I ran.

I ran out the door of the bathroom and then quickly out the East Wing entrance to the upper-grade playground. I stopped and looked back to see if he was following me. He was only like ten feet behind me and closing the distance quickly. I panicked and ran down the hill leading to the football field.

I could hear Staples right behind me, growling like a rabid dog. When I got to the bottom, I crouched and grabbed a handful of gravel. I spun around while back-pedaling and threw it into his face. He yelled and turned away from me.

I kicked into high gear and headed toward the street. I knew it would not take long for him to catch me on foot, but if I could just get somewhere more visible to passing cars . . .

I didn't even get close. His legs were longer and stronger. I had gotten only thirty yards down the football field when I felt someone shove me hard in the back, and I went sprawling onto the ground, my elbow scraping over the dry fall grass. It burned and the wind got knocked right out of me. I felt my elbow moisten with blood as I tried to catch my breath.

But then he was on me. He grabbed my shirt and lifted me off the ground easily. I could have kicked him or something, but I was too busy trying to get some air into my lungs. I wheezed as he carried me by my shirt collar back toward the parking lot.

As I finally caught my breath, Staples set me on my feet. His hand moved from my shirt to the back of my neck, where it clamped down so hard I thought my head was going to fall off.

"Don't try to run again or you're dead," he whispered in my ear. He guided me toward his red sports car. "Now get in."

He opened the passenger door to the red sports car and I did as I was told, fear swelling inside of me like a teacup being filled with a garden hose. I'd never been more scared in my whole life. I was too scared to even try to think of a way out of this.

He got in the car and started driving. I had no idea where he was headed, but it was out near the edge of town. He headed past the Walmart and just kept going. I looked out the window as a farm field passed by. I kept imagining Staples making me dig my own grave out in some farmer's deserted cow pasture. Imagining your own death has a way of making you feel pretty sick.

Chapter 26

After driving in silence for a few minutes, Staples took out his phone.

"Yeah, PJ. I need you to meet me out at the Yard. We've got something to take care of."

I heard PJ's muffled reply but couldn't make out the words.

"I don't care who's over at your house. This is more important than any girl, you idiot. Now get the other three and get out here!" I couldn't be sure, but behind it all I thought I heard uncertainty or maybe even fear in Staples's voice.

So we were going to the Yard. The Yard is this vacant dirt lot a few miles out of town where teenagers go to scare themselves to death on Halloween and drink themselves passed-out on other Saturday nights. Vince's brother had told us about it. It's full of junk and weeds and old cars and nobody cares enough about it to ever go out there and clean up. As far as I know, nobody even knows who owns the land. Rumor was that they were going to build a bunch of houses out there but had to stop because the land is supposedly haunted. I guess when they started digging up the land, a bunch of bad stuff happened. Like, the machines stopped working and it rained a lot, but it rained only out in the Yard and nowhere else. Also, supposedly accidents kept happening and the workers were getting hurt and hearing voices and stuff. I never did believe those stories. Still, you couldn't have paid me to go out to the Yard alone in the middle of the night.

I did think it was fitting that I would probably end up haunting the place myself pretty soon. It was partially my fault; this was the business I'd chosen. But I wasn't ready to just give up, not by a long shot.

I shifted in my seat.

"Don't try anything." Staples said. "Stop moving so much."

After a few more minutes he turned the car on to a gravel road. Then after about a hundred feet he turned into a massive dirt lot. There was garbage littered all around, and a few abandoned cars rested under some trees on the far side of the dirt clearing. We were at the Yard. It looked just like I'd heard: a stretch of land that had been leveled for construction years ago and then was just abandoned overnight. Maybe those ghost rumors weren't just rumors after all.

Staples got out of the car. He opened my door, pulled me out, and dragged me across the hard, hot dirt by my foot. He stopped about thirty feet away from the car and dropped my leg. I was pretty sure my back had gotten all scratched up, but I was so scared I barely noticed.

"What do you have to say now, Christian?" He smirked.

"Nice car," I said, figuring that going out a smart-mouth would be much cooler than as a whimpering crybaby.

Staples didn't get mad, though. Instead he laughed as he sat down on an old tire. I was just starting to realize that he laughed a lot.

We waited in silence for a while. I sat on the ground and squinted up at some clouds. Maybe he wouldn't kill me after all. I mean, that would be pretty ridiculous. Then again, what else could happen? One thing was sure: I was on my own. None of my crew knew where I was and I had no way to tell them. Even if they did call the cops, they'd never find us out here.

Eventually PJ's black Honda came crackling into the Yard. PJ and the other three high school kids climbed out and walked over to us.

"Jeez, Staples, what is this?" PJ said, sounding a little annoyed and shocked.

"I've caught us a little troublemaker! He tried to blackmail me, and now we're going to make him pay," Staples said.

"You kidnapped a little kid?" said one of the teen-agers, laughing. But he didn't really sound all that amused.

Staples shrugged.

"What are you going to do with him?" PJ asked.

"You mean, what are *we* going to do with him, right?" Staples asked with a glare so dark that his eyes were like two black holes.

"Uh, yeah, sure, whatever . . ." PJ said, sounding nervous.

"Are you going soft on me, PJ?" Staples asked. "Huh? You had no problem beating him up after he kicked you. Am I supposed to just sit here and do nothing when he goes after me? Is that how it is? You know what's in this for me; I can't let him do that."

I wondered what Staples had meant by that. What didn't I know about his business that was so important to him?

Staples stood up and walked over to PJ. I thought he was going to punch him, and I think PJ did, too, because he flinched. But Staples just slapped him across the back like they were old friends.

"Come on, man!" Staples said with a big grin. "You're still in this with me, right?"

PJ hesitated. I couldn't really see from my angle, but I think Staples gave him a look that pleaded for agreement. Staples had usually seemed so in control, but now he was acting almost desperate.

"Yeah, you're right," PJ finally said.

"All right, that's my boy!" Staples said, punching his arm. PJ winced in pain. "Just remember who pays for your car's upgrades and your girlfriend's necklaces and stuff, right?"

PJ nodded and tried to laugh.

Staples turned to face me. He was still smiling.

"I guess it's about that time, Christian," he said, walking over to me. "What do you say we get this show on the road?"

"Actually, I could stand to wait a little bit," I said.

He laughed. Then he said, "Oh, Christian. I really did like you, you know? You're a funny kid. We maybe even could have been friends."

He loomed over me, looking like the devil himself. I think he was waiting for me to say something else. I just looked up at him with the meanest glare I could manage.

"No last words? Just a nasty look?" he asked.

I stayed silent.

"Okay, then, suit yourself," he said as he cracked his knuckles. It sounded like bones snapping. I winced as he cracked each finger one by one.

I didn't really like where this whole thing was headed.

Chapter 27

Staples looked down at me for a few moments. The sun was almost directly behind his head, and his face just appeared as a black silhouette. Even though I couldn't see it, I was pretty sure he was smiling. Then he reached down and grabbed the collar of my shirt and lifted me into the air.

I twisted around to see if his posse was really going to let him do this, and that's when I saw perhaps the greatest sight I've ever seen. There was a bike gang headed our way down the gravel road. The bikes may have been pedal bicycles and not huge chopper motorcycles, and they were ridden by a bunch of kids instead of big muscular dudes with tattoos and black leather, but to me it was all the same at that point.

The caravan consisted of six riders. In the lead was a really little kid on a small bike. As they drew nearer, I was finally able to make out who it was: Fred. Fred was leading the charge, and behind him rode Vince, Joe, Nubby, Great White, and Kitten.

Staples dropped me to the ground and turned to face the newcomers.

"What the . . ."

Everybody turned as the six bikes skidded to a stop in quick succession on the dirt. It was really cool as the dirt sprayed up in front of them. Then Nubby, the last one to stop, accidentally went too far and his front wheel hit Joe's bike, and he toppled off and sprawled onto the ground headfirst. It kind of ruined the moment a little bit. The four high school kids laughed, but Staples just stared as Nubby quickly climbed back to his feet.

"What do we have here? A dork convention?" one of the high school kids said, and then laughed. Nobody else laughed with him.

I think they might have been too busy warily eyeing what I had just noticed: my six rescuers had weapons strapped across their backs. But as they dismounted their bikes and armed themselves, I noticed that they didn't exactly bring *real* weapons. Vince, for instance, had a plastic snow shovel. Fred held a long, skinny tree branch out in front of him, but in all honesty, it was just a gnarly twig that would probably shatter if hit by a light breeze. Joe had one of those thick foam noodles that kids sometimes bring to the swimming pool. Nubby held a giant rubber trout with a missing dorsal fin and bite marks all over it as if he'd gotten hungry and chewed on it during the bike ride.

At least Great White had a gun. The only problem was that it was a water gun. I especially questioned his choice of weapon. It's not like Staples was a witch who'd melt when sprayed with water. But then again, Great White was there to help me, they all were, and that's what mattered most. Kitten was the only one who looked like he was used to picking out effective weapons. He had a really nasty-looking, rusty lawn rake. That didn't surprise me; you could always count on Kitten to bring a flamethrower to roast a marshmallow.

My friends lined up in front of us about twenty feet away. Staples stood with PJ and the other three high school kids between my rescuers and me.

The searing sun shone on a classic showdown. I was so proud of my crew. I didn't know how they'd done it, but they'd somehow found out where I was and then rode out the few miles on their bikes. And now they were apparently ready to fight for me. Even if they weren't really equipped for it.

The two sides stared at each other. The only noise was

that of a few birds singing about whatever they had to sing about. Then finally the silence was broken.

"Let him go, Staples." It was Vince.

"Or what, you'll beat me up with your little toys?" Staples said with a smirk.

"Umm, yeah, kind of. I guess that's what would happen," Vince said.

He never is too good at confrontations, like I've said before.

"You'll be sorry if you hurt him, Staples," Nubby said, looking pretty intimidating for a seventh grader holding a rubber trout.

"Oooh, will I?" Staples said with a sneer.

That's when Kitten did what Kitten does best: something crazy. He walked a few steps over to the black Honda with the huge spoiler. He raised the rake above his head. He held it there for a moment while everyone watched.

Then he slammed it onto the roof of the car. In the empty Yard the clang was deafening.

"No!" PJ screamed. I heard some of his buddies say things that would've made my mom faint.

Kitten dragged the rake across the roof, and the screeching noise made us all wince and grit our teeth. Except for Staples—he just stood there smiling. Kitten finished and the screeches faded. It was hard to see from my spot, but we all knew there were some nasty scratches on the car. One of the most disturbing smiles I'd ever seen spread slowly across Kitten's face like an expanding pool of blood. I think the rest of us in the Yard got chills up our spines all at the same time.

PJ made a move to go after Kitten, but the little psycho raised the rake again.

"Stay where you are or I'll do the back window next," he said in his small, quiet voice. PJ complied as if he was being barked at by a drill instructor. Kitten's arms shook slightly, not from nerves I don't think but from excitement. He *wanted* PJ to keep coming at him so he could smash the back window.

"Now let him go or we'll make that car look like a piece of Swiss cheese," Nubby said.

Staples laughed. He rocked back on his heels and then shook his head.

"Go ahead, do it. I don't care," he said.

There was a dead silence. I think my crew didn't really know what to do.

Then Kitten shrugged and raised the rake again. "Okay, we will."

"Wait!" PJ yelled. "Wait. You know what? I'm out of here. Don't hurt my baby. I need it; just . . ." He took car keys from his pocket and moved toward the car. He opened the driver's side door.

"Yeah, I'm going to go, too, Staples. I got a baseball scholarship, you know?" said another of the high school kids.

"Yeah, I don't really want to get my nose raked off by some psycho little kid. I got a pretty face, right?" said the high school kid with spiky blond hair. "Sorry, Staples."

The three of them got into the black Honda. The car backed up into the gravel road and then sped away, leaving a trail of dust behind it. Staples stared at it silently.

"Let him go, Staples. You're outnumbered," Vince said.

My men all took a few steps toward Staples.

That's when he hauled me up by my shirt again. He wrapped an arm around my neck and squeezed. I struggled to breathe, and I felt the blood rush to my face. His other hand took out his phone and he flipped it open.

"What are you doing?" Vince asked.

"I'm calling in an anonymous tip," Staples said calmly.

"To who?" Vince asked, looking a little worried.

"Here's the thing," Staples said as his fingers pressed the keys on his phone. "Everyone thinks you're all so perfect. That I'm a delinquent and you're just these saints when, in fact, we're not all that different. But now they're all going to see you for what you really are—just a bunch of scheming, greedy, rich kids with too much time and no accountability."

I didn't like where this was headed.

"Yeah, I'd like to speak to Principal Dickerson," Staples said into the phone. "Sure, I'll hold."

Staples's arm stayed gripped around my neck. Not too hard that I couldn't breathe, but it hurt.

"Wait, Staples, maybe we can work something out," Vince said, panic rising in his voice. He knew as well as I did that if Staples directed Dickerson to our office in the East Wing bathroom we'd all be expelled.

"Oh yeah?" Staples said. "I doubt it."

I looked at my would-be rescuers. They looked at each other, unsure of what to do. I didn't see Great White. During the commotion he had somehow snuck off. I hoped Staples wouldn't notice. And that whatever Great White was doing, he had a plan.

"We can start negotiating by you telling me where you took my money," Staples said.

Everybody seemed unsure of what to do next. Vince also knew he couldn't tell him that, because then Staples would likely still turn us in and we'd lose our leverage. I relaxed a little bit. I was going to conserve my energy.

Vince stepped forward as the others stepped back. He held up his hands in front of him.

"Look, Staples, don't do anything crazy, okay? Let's just talk about this. We didn't actually kidnap your dog; he's just fine, okay?" Vince said.

"Oops, too late," Staples said. "The secretary is connecting me now."

We all waited and I don't think anybody breathed. So this was it. It was all over.

"Yeah, Mr. Dickerson?" Staples said into the phone. My head was close to Staples from where I was, and I heard Dickerson's unmistakable voice faintly from somewhere above me. Staples wasn't bluffing; he really had called the school. "Yeah, I want to report some—"

That's when Great White struck. I heard a soft whizzing noise and then felt liquid splash onto my face. It may have been only water from Great White's squirt gun, but it had surprised Staples just enough for him to loosen his grip on me ever so slightly. That was all I needed. I threw an elbow into his side, and he dropped me completely.

"*Ow!*" He grabbed his ribs as I rolled away from him.

I heard his phone hit the ground, and then the others were upon him.

"Don't move!" Nubby yelled.

Staples tried to run, but Kitten got him first.

I heard Kitten's squeal of a battle cry as he picked up his weapon, ready to rake Staples's face like it was a pile of leaves. He lunged with the handle end first, and the heavy wood cracked against Staples's kneecap. Staples hit the dirt hard and rolled to his back, moaning.

I picked up his phone and hit the disconnect button while my crew surrounded him. I thought they were going to tenderize Staples like a choice-cut sirloin, the way they were approaching him. He was holding his knee where Kitten had hit him, but otherwise he looked calm. Unafraid—like a kid who's already sunk lower than the punishment of a physical beating.

"Let us take him out, Mac. He's a lying sack of—" Kitten started.

"Hang on," I interrupted. "We're not going to stoop to that level."

In truth, it wasn't about stooping or not. I looked at Vince, and he had the strangest expression on his face, like he was miles away from this place. Then Vince looked right at me and I saw it. Even with everything that had happened, he felt truly bad for Staples. After all, Vince knew what that was like: to have to give money to parents and not to have a dad around. Staples's and Vince's situations weren't all that different, and they had grown up right near each other their whole lives. But still, we somehow had to make sure he wasn't going to turn us in to Dickerson the first chance he got. We couldn't just let him go.

"Look, Staples," I said. "I understand that you did all this because of your family situation. You're trying to help out your dad. But that doesn't—"

"You don't know anything," Staples interrupted. He didn't sound mad, though, just empty. "I'm not doing any of this for my loser dad."

I waited for him to continue, and after a short silence, he did.

"I'm doing all of this for my sister."

Of course. The picture I had seen in his office. He had looked just like a regular kid in that picture. I guess there was a time when he had been different, when things were better for him.

"My sister," he repeated. He wasn't talking directly at me or anybody. He was looking at the ground as if the dirt could talk back or would understand what he was going through. "She was taken from us a few years ago. She lives with a foster family now. I'm only trying to help my dad get back on his feet so I can get my sister back for us. For me. But my dad, he just doesn't seem to care."

I didn't know what to say. None of us did. So we waited for him to continue. But when he finally did, some life had come back to him and he looked right at me, his face full of anger, but whether he was really mad at me or at his dad I wasn't sure. Maybe both.

"All you rich kids. Kids like you who have everything. You just don't get how easy you have it. You get every-thing, you have everything, you don't even think twice about it. You just go through life and there's always stuff there, and family there, and you have everything so easily and you don't even get it."

"I used to live right near you, Staples. At Bella Vista trailer park, don't you remember? We even played football together a few times."

Staples shook his head slightly and squinted up at me. "Don't remember and don't care to, Richie McMoney-Bags."

I sighed.

"I'm not rich, Staples," I said, but my words sounded empty.

Because he was right. I may have *used* to live near him in the same trailer park, but now I did have it a lot easier than he did. Of course it was easier for me to run a clean, successful business when I had no other worries in life and all of the money I made could go right back into the business. And I had a real family; I couldn't imagine what it would be like without them. I was rich. And he wasn't, and I had rubbed it in his face earlier in my office. He hardly had a family, didn't seem to have any real friends, and had a failing, corrupt business. No wonder he hated me so much.

I looked at Vince again. He looked back at me. But he didn't have to—I knew already what I needed to do. This kid on the ground in front of me, who had tried to destroy my life, deserved some pro bono services.

"Look, Staples, how about we team up after all? I mean, not like in a cheesy way where we're now like best friends who hold hands and sing pop songs together while prancing through the meadow. But more so I'll be your business adviser. I can help you run your business better; I can help you make more money. The right way. I'll even start you off with a business loan. We'll get your sister back for you."

"I don't need your help," he said, scoffing. "She's my sister. I'm her brother. I can get her back on my own."

I sighed and looked at Vince again. He just shrugged.

"Well, if you ever change your mind, you know where to find me," I said. "In the meantime I'm going to need to keep some of the stuff we found in your shed as collateral. The notebooks detailing bets you took and other records that might prompt the authorities to look further into any other unsavory activities you might have going on. If you ever tip off Dickerson, then we'll have to tip off the cops about what you've been up to, and then you'll never get your sister back."

He glared at me.

"Hey, I don't want it to be like this. But I clearly can't trust you without any insurance," I said. "I offered my help and you turned it down, so this is what we're left with."

"Yeah, whatever, Christian," Staples said. "Keep that stuff, I don't care. I'm not going to say anything to anybody." He dropped his head again, making no effort to get up. He just ran his hand through the dirt as if digging for the answer to all his problems.

There was still an edge to his voice I didn't so much care for, but I could tell he wasn't going to fight anymore. He looked about as defeated and hopeless as the Cubs were of ever winning the World Series.

"The name's Mac, by the way," I said to him.

"Whatever, *Mac*," he said without looking up.

"We're not actually going to let him go, are we?" Kitten asked. I could tell he still wanted more payback for the Shed incident. I would have to make it up to him with money once I got my Funds back in my hands.

"Yes. It's not worth the trouble. Plus, he clearly hasn't gotten too many breaks in his life. Everybody needs a break once in a while."

Staples scoffed at this, but I think it was more in agreement with what I'd said than anything else.

"Let's go," I said.

We all walked back to the bikes. Staples just sat there on the ground staring at the dirt with a blank look in his eyes. He looked like a broken toy.

"By the way," I said as we approached the bikes. "What's with all your weapons? You couldn't find anything that might've actually scared them?"

Nubby laughed and waved the trout chew toy at me. "Hey, we were in a hurry. This was the only stuff we could find in Staples's shed on such short notice."

Great White came running out from behind a nearby tree now that it was clear the conflict was over.

"I owe you," I said.

"Bloody right you do," he said, and laughed. "A few thousand quid ought to do it."

I chuckled, too, even though I knew he wasn't kidding. I was going to have to pay him a pretty hefty sum for what he'd done for me. I wasn't really sure how many dollars a few thousand quid would be, though. It must have been another one of those British things.

"Why the heck did you decide to bring a water gun, anyway?" I asked.

Great White laughed. "Hey, it worked, didn't it, mate?"

I grinned and nodded. He had a point. I couldn't really argue; that dumb water gun had probably saved my business, my permanent record, and my reputation.

Before we left, I went to Staples's car and grabbed his car keys from the ignition. I shoved them into my pocket and then stood on the pegs on the back wheels of Vince's bike. I grabbed his backpack to steady myself.

"Let's go," I said, and we rode.

Chapter **28**

It took a good thirty minutes to get back to our neighborhood. On the way I asked for more details about the raid. In addition to finding the Emergency Fund and the Game Fund under the floorboards, they'd also found the same extensive logs that Tyrell and I had found Saturday of bets placed and money taken and kids who Staples had paid off to throw games. Oddly enough, they hadn't found much money besides what he had stolen from me. My crew had left all the records and money back at Vince's house with Tyrell guarding them. We'd store all of Staples's records in a safe place for insurance, just in case he ever tried to come back. And we'd divvy up whatever extra money they did find to all the kids he'd swindled it from.

They also told me how they found out we were at the Yard. After the phone cut out they grabbed whatever weapons they could find and went to the school to check things out. There they found Fred curled up into a little ball. He must have been feeling pretty guilty because as soon as they got him unfurled, Fred told them that Staples usually brought people who needed to be taught a lesson out to the Yard. They jumped back on their bikes and rode on out to save me.

Everybody was sweating pretty hard by the time we got back into town. I thanked them all at least a billion times and told them to meet me in my office at morning recess. After we parted ways, I had Vince ride to Staples's house. I went onto the porch and tossed his car keys inside the mailbox.

Then we rode to my house. Once in my driveway I hopped off the bike and faced Vince. He looked at me, squinting into the sun.

"Hey, Mac, I'm glad you're okay. I was pretty worried there for a while," he said.

"Yeah, me, too. Thanks for rescuing me."

"Hey, no problem. It's like my grandma always says, 'A real friend is someone who is there for you when he'd rather be anywhere else.'"

I smiled. "Hey, that one's pretty good. She really says that?"

"No, of course not. I made some changes. Hers goes something like this: 'A friend is like an eagle with no wings because they'll both get eaten by a giant spaghetti noodle.'"

We both laughed.

"Hey, why didn't you guys ever call the cops?" I asked.

"We didn't really know for sure if you really were out at the Yard. Plus, the bullies didn't want the cops around to witness the sort of revenge that they were planning," Vince said.

"Makes sense," I said with a shrug. "Hey, Vince?"

"Yeah?"

"I'm sorry again that I actually thought that you were the traitor for a while. It was horrible to have believed it," I said. I looked at him, not knowing what else to say.

He shook his head. "Remember a few years ago when I was so convinced that you stole my Ron Santo rookie card because you just happened to buy one on the same day that mine went missing? I was so mad at you that I wouldn't even look at you, let alone talk to you. Yet, when I found my card a few days later, you forgave me instantly. You weren't even mad that I suspected you. So now I figure that I should do the same."

"I still feel bad, that's all," I said.

"I'm just glad you're still alive. And that we got all our money back and that we're still friends and business partners and stuff like that." He rolled his bike's front tire back and forth across a line on the sidewalk.

"Me, too. That was like the worst three days of my life," I said as I scratched my eye. I thought I'd gotten some sand in it while I was on the ground out at the Yard.

"Hey, you're not going to get all weepy on me, are you?" Vince said.

"No, no it was just—"

"Because it's totally okay if you do," Vince interrupted. "I've actually been collecting tears. I'm planning on building a time machine that runs on tears, bleach, and oranges. Then I can go way back and tell the Cubs not to trade away Greg Maddux and draft Mark Prior. Oh, it would also be cool to, like, see the Gettysburg Address or something, too."

He had stepped off his bike and was now holding a little clear tube up to my cheek. He had a serious look on his face, as if missing a single tear would mean the end of the world.

I pushed his hand away. He had such perfect timing.

"Come on! Get out of here with that," I said. "Where did you get that anyways? How long have you been carrying that vial around, waiting for a time like this?"

Vince laughed. "We did a dumb science lab today in Hanson's class. I stole it. Don't you believe me? Start crying, please."

I shoved him back a little again and said, "I can get a few going if you give me some space, you needy creep."

"No, I'm just messing around, Mac. It's too late to save the Cubs of the past, and the Gettysburg Address would be totally boring, I bet." He chucked the little vial into the garbage can on the curb. "But I do have a good one for you. For real this time. I thought of it back when Staples had you in a headlock, but I figured that wasn't the best time to ask."

"Yeah, no kidding. All right, let's have it," I said.

"Who was the first Cub to win the Rookie of the Year award?"

"Oh man . . . that is tough . . . Ernie Banks?"

"I can't believe it. I've finally defeated Mac. I am the new Cubs fan champion!" Vince yelled as he raised his arms into the air. "You're close, but the answer is Billy Williams in 1961."

I staggered backward and shook my head. "I declare shenanigans! Get the broom; it's not legal to ask a question right after I was just in a near-death experience!" I yelled, but I was laughing, too.

"Okay, okay, fine. I'll give you a pass this *one* time, being that you just about got a back-alley spinal adjustment a few minutes ago. But I will get you again, Mac," Vince said while grinning.

"We'll see about that. Speaking of the Cubs, are we

still going to the game?" I asked. I knew this was kind of a tricky question now, since Vince's family needed money so badly. I mean, is it that easy to give up a once-in-a-lifetime opportunity that you had dreamed about for your whole life? Could we go to a game costing thousands of dollars in good conscience while Vince's mom sat at home and wasted away talking about the pros and cons of Swedish politics with a switched-off TV?

"Well, in case you forgot, the Cubs are up three games to none over the Phillies. So if they win tonight, the tickets will go on sale tomorrow morning. The sooner we try for them the better, since they'll be out of our price range probably by tomorrow night," Vince said.

"Why don't you come over and we'll watch the game together? And if they win, we'll figure it out right then and there."

"All right, sounds good," he said, and rode off down the street.

It wasn't that simple, though. I had seen the look in his eyes. It was just a glimmer, but it was there: uncertainty. He had been thinking the same thing I had. Could we really spend close to six thousand dollars on one baseball game when his family was in such bad shape? I guessed we'd have to talk about it that night as we watched the game.

It was almost a sure thing, too. Very few teams in

baseball history had ever lost a 3–0 lead in a Champion-ship Series. It was as close as a sure thing as you could get in baseball. Just the thought that the Cubs were that close to finally making it back sent shivers up my spine. But right then I wasn't sure if it *was* because of the Cubs that I felt so happy. I think it was due more to the fact that I had regained my business, my money, and most important, my best friend.

I went straight to the bathroom and cleaned up. My elbow and back had some pretty good scrapes, but oth-erwise the damage wasn't too bad. My parents didn't even notice that anything was wrong by the time we all sat down for dinner. I tried not to laugh too much as I sat there eating my mom's chili. I kept wondering what my parents would think if they knew what had happened to me after school. It all seemed pretty funny now that it was over.

Chapter 29

The next morning at recess we all grouped in my office. I thanked everyone with a pretty good chunk of the Emergency Fund. I told Tyrell and the three bullies that I'd never forget what they had done and anytime they needed something they should feel free to stop by my office. They left the East Wing boys' bathroom much, much richer than they had been before they'd entered.

"Well, Fred, I have to say thanks," I said after the others left. "I mean, you *did* betray us all, but what you did to make up for it took a lot of guts."

"No, Mac. I'm still really sorry for that. I mean, Staples can be pretty mean and I was way too scared to say no to him most of the time," he said. "I really hated lying all the time, I really did, but my other option was to get beat up. Badly."

Speaking of Staples, you might be wondering what exactly happened to him. Well, nobody's really sure. He just kind of disappeared. We rode by his house on our bikes a few days after the incident at the Yard and it was completely abandoned, red tape all across the doors and windows. A few weeks later the house had been cleaned up a little bit and a bright white For Sale sign sat in the front lawn looking like a used car salesman standing next to a lot of rusty bicycles.

I wasn't sure if Staples had run because he was afraid of my threats to turn him in to the cops, or if it was out of shame, or maybe his dad had gotten arrested and Staples was living with foster parents like his sister was. I didn't know, and I didn't care so much, except I did hope that wherever he was, he was in a better place. And I really, truly hoped that he got his sister back someday. Maybe that's all he really needed to get himself back on the right track. Because deep down, I'm not sure he was all that bad a guy. Maybe I had pushed his buttons a little bit. The last time I saw him was back in the Yard, when he was just sitting there staring at the ground.

With the Staples mess officially taken care of, my first order of business was to make amends with a former employee. I'd never wrongfully fired somebody before, and Brady didn't deserve that kind of embarrassment. So I called him into my office and offered him a heartfelt apology. And a nice bonus.

You might also be wondering about the Cubs game, too, I bet. As I said before, we were in kind of a predicament, given our access to loads of cash and Vince's family having a real hard time right then. And it would have been almost impossible to have to choose, but luckily for us we never had to. Because the Cubs chose for us by doing what they do best: choking.

That's right, the Cubs choked away their last four games and became one of just a few teams to ever lose a 3–0 lead in a Championship Series. So they missed the World Series yet again, which honestly shouldn't have surprised anybody. It's like one of those things that are written in some dusty prophecy that old, creepy guys in robes will talk about for years to come while sitting in a circle surrounded by candles and incense. So let it be written, so let it be sealed in fate: *The Cubs will be losers forever.*

But I'm not bitter, oh no. Definitely not bitter. I mean, I give them my blood, sweat, and tears and they repay me with year after year of losing seasons. Why should I be bitter? Okay, okay, I'm still a little pissed about the whole thing; it was pretty devastating. Vince even cried a little bit. But like I said, what else is new? I've already said they're the worst team in sports history. Losing is like breathing for them—it comes naturally. They don't even have to think about it; it just happens. Every time. No matter what.

But the one bright side was that it freed up some money for Vince to sneakily give to his mom in small amounts. And we still have a pretty good head start now for saving up for next year. The odds of the Cubs being that good two years in a row are astronomically high, but it's all us Cubs fans have. Hope.

With the news of Staples's demise, it didn't take long at all for our business to get back on track. Most kids didn't know that Staples had moved away. The rumor that most kids seemed to believe was that we had buried Staples alive out in the Yard and now his ghost haunted the place. I have to say that that's a pretty gruesome thought, but you have to hand it to the kids at my school: they have pretty good imaginations. Anyways, kids began pouring in and some were there simply to be able to say they talked to the guys who had defeated Staples. It was all kind of embarrassing, to be honest.

Joe stayed on as my strongman, and Vince went back to managing the finances and just being generally brilliant and hilarious. And we also added one more guy to the payroll. It took some time for us all to trust him fully, but eventually Fred proved to be a great addition. He is now the official record keeper. He sits in the stall next to mine and takes notes on his Nintendo DS. We have a pretty good system, and business was positively booming within days of the Staples Incident.

Things really were going well. In fact, they couldn't have been going any better. At least, that is until *she* walked into my office on one rainy Tuesday afternoon. I knew she was trouble from the moment I laid eyes on her. Everyone knows that in grade school, girls are more dangerous than shotguns. At least that's if shotguns are as dangerous as Officer Weston told us they are that one day he came to our class to tell us about how if you basically even looked at a shotgun, then you'd end up a smelly, homeless bum who failed out of school and lost all your friends and family and all that you'd have left in the whole world was a one-armed teddy bear named Oscar.

She walked into my office with damp hair and a swagger that I found both attractive and unnerving. She was tall and impossibly pretty. I didn't even know if I was making sense when I started talking to her. But it didn't matter, because she quickly took over the conversation. Her voice was intelligent and confident and it didn't take long for her to entangle me in a web of brutal lies and problems so complicated that I was sure my head would explode.

But that's probably a story better left for another day.

ACKNOWLEDGMENTS

Thanks to the following for all of their help and support: Chris Richman, Theodore Quester, Ruta Sepetys, Mark McVeigh, Mike Rylander, my parents, the Debs, Tenners, and Elevensies, and everyone at HarperCollins and Walden Media. Thanks to my editor, Jordan Brown, for making this book better than I ever thought it could be. Thanks to my agent, Steven Malk, for everything; this book truly would not exist without you. Also important were my beard, it knows why, and cheese, for being really tasty. Finally, thank you to my best friend and beautiful wife, Amanda, who makes everything possible.